Faulty
Predictions

FLANNERY
O'CONNOR
AWARD
FOR
SHORT
FICTION

Nancy Zafris,
Series Editor

Faulty Predictions

....

Stories by Karin Lin-Greenberg

....

The University of Georgia Press
Athens and London

"A Good Brother" © 2010 by the Antioch Review, Inc.,
first appeared in the Antioch Review, vol. 68, no. 3.
Reprinted by permission of the editors.

"Miller Duskman's Mistakes" © 2014 by the Antioch Review, Inc.,
first appeared in the Antioch Review, vol. 72, no. 3.
Reprinted by permission of the editors.

Designed by Kaelin Chappell Broaddus
Set in 10.5/14 Filosofia Regular by Kaelin Chappell Broaddus
Printed and bound by Sheridan Books, Inc.
The paper in this book meets the guidelines for
permanence and durability of the Committee on
Production Guidelines for Book Longevity of the
Council on Library Resources.

Most University of Georgia Press titles are
available from popular e-book vendors.

Printed in the United States of America
14 15 16 17 18 c 5 4 3 2 1

Library of Congress Cataloging-in-Publication Data
Lin-Greenberg, Karin.
[Short stories. Selections]
Faulty predictions / Karin Lin-Greenberg.
pages cm — (Flannery O'Connor Award for Short Fiction)
ISBN 978-0-8203-4686-1 (hardback)
I. Title.
PS3612.I52F38   2014
813'.6—dc23
2014019832

British Library Cataloging-in-Publication Data available

*For my parents
and
for my brother, Erik*

Contents

Acknowledgments

The following stories appeared in slightly different forms in other publications: "Editorial Decisions" in *Cutthroat*, "Prized Possessions" in *Epoch*, "Designated Driver" (as "Care") in *Kenyon Review Online*, "The Local Scrooge" (as "What Was There Long Ago") in *North American Review*, "Bread" in *Berkeley Fiction Review*, and "A Good Brother" and "Miller Duskman's Mistakes" in *Antioch Review*. I am grateful to the editors of the journals who first published these stories, especially to Geeta Kothari at the *Kenyon Review*. My sincere thanks to the staff at the University of Georgia Press for their dedication and care in ushering this book into the world. I am especially grateful to Nancy Zafris, series editor for the Flannery O'Connor Award, for her generosity with her time, good advice, and editorial wisdom. Thank you to my family; I am fortunate to belong to a family that has encouraged all my creative endeavors throughout the years. Thank you also to my many teachers and colleagues—from Pennsylvania to Missouri to Ohio to North Carolina to New York—who have provided me with guidance and support. Finally, big thanks to Jeff Janssens, who always helps me out with details related to sports in my stories, for his willingness to give me thoughtful feedback on my writing, even on days when he has seventy-five student essays to grade, and for his encouragement and belief.

Faulty
Predictions

....

Editorial Decisions

....

W e were fifteen, sixteen, seventeen. We met on Wednesday afternoons at 3 p.m. in the squishy orange chairs in the corner of the
school library where the sun streamed in through large windows. We
were an editorial board, and we liked this term very much—we thought
of how good it would look on our college applications under the word
"Activities." That year we named our literary magazine *Semicolon*; we
found beauty in the semicolon, which we deemed underused and un-
derappreciated, especially by our classmates, the ones who couldn't
tell the difference between a colon and a semicolon if their lives depended on it. Soon we would be off to Georgetown and Dartmouth and
Wellesley and Stanford. We would become English majors. We gos-
siped about how our classmates, those who never properly grasped
English grammar, would go to large, overcrowded state schools.

This is how our magazine worked: we accepted anonymous submissions from students in our school, we took turns reading the submissions aloud, then we discussed them and voted on what we would
allow into our magazine. Somehow every issue contained mostly work
by the editorial board. "It's completely fair," we said. "The submissions are read anonymously." Yet we could always sense when a sub-
mission had been written by one of us—maybe because the author
got suddenly quiet, stared at the rest of the editorial board with wide,
expectant eyes, nervously rocked back and forth until a decision had
been made. But we told ourselves the magazine consisted of mostly

our own work because our writing was just better, more vivid, cut closer to the soul than everyone else's.

There were words we liked, words we sought out in the submissions: malaise, chaos, ennui, angst, brokenhearted. Here is the first poem we accepted for the fall issue:

My brokenhearted heart
beats
onward
like a soldier
m-a-r-c-h-i-n-g
and I wonder
how many
more
years
of
this
chaos
my soul
can
endure.

We knew brilliance when we saw it. We gasped at the poignancy, the universality of the message. We especially liked the word choice.

Later, when we went to college, we learned to love other words: patriarchy, Foucault, hegemony, Derrida, pastiche, postmodern. We loved the word "postmodern." It was like a Swiss Army knife, good for helping us out of jams, multipurpose. Examples: (1) "You don't understand my student documentary film because it's postmodern. It's not meant to be understood." (2) "*Moby-Dick* is a very postmodern novel employing the technique of pastiche." (3) "No, Mother, I did not learn to dress like a hobo at college. This mismatching is an intentional postmodern statement."

Each fall, we needed to replace the seniors on our staff whom we'd lost to college. This is how we chose: we asked all interested parties to write a three-page essay about a story or poem that was in the last issue of our magazine. We asked for a close critical analysis, but what we really wanted, what we were hungry for, was praise; we wanted to hear that we'd put together a magazine that rivaled the *New Yorker*. Unlike our submissions, these applications were not submitted anonymously. We wanted to make sure each person we chose was qualified in every way; we wanted to make sure our new members would truly fit in.

One afternoon in early September we met to choose two new members to join the editorial board. There were nineteen applications to go through. We felt powerful, easily dismissing essays we found too simplistic, too narrow-minded, too full of flowery prose. We were especially critical of spelling errors; we shook our heads and declared that spell-check can't help you if you are, in general, an idiot. We spent an hour tossing applications into a growing pile in the center of our circle, and then we came across a stunningly good essay.

The essay was written by one of the two boys in the long black trench coats. They were boys who always looked sullen and miserable and had pale, acne-speckled skin. They dyed their hair the color of coal. The two boys in the trench coats were always together; we'd never seen one without the other. We could barely tell them apart.

The boys always came into the library when we had our editorial board meetings. They sat at a table in the far corner of the library, the darkest part, where no sun shone in. They read comic books that we thought were from Japan. We'd caught glimpses of the violent and bloody covers. "What a cliché," we said, staring at their trench coats. "If they want to be so different, they shouldn't dress like every other depressed kid in America." Depression was OK, encouraged even, in poetry; in real life, people who were depressed bored us.

On the day the editorial board met to select our new members, half of the boys' lacrosse team had detention in the library. They were in their uniforms, ready to run out to the field as soon as detention was over. They sat in a pack at one of the big oak tables, tilting back in their chairs, laughing. Every few minutes, they got too noisy and were shushed by a librarian. Soon after, they'd grow noisy again. They held their sticks over their shoulders, and when the detention monitor wasn't looking, they leaned back and poked the boys in the trench coats with their lacrosse sticks. "Hey, freakshows," the lacrosse boys said, "give us your comic books." The boys in the trench coats ignored the lacrosse players.

One lacrosse player tried to poke a trench coat boy again; the other trench coat boy put his hand on his friend's back, blocking the stick. We knew this was unacceptable: there was no touching between boys in high school unless it was absolutely necessary in an athletic event. We knew there would be consequences, and we saw anger flush the faces of the lacrosse players.

"Fags," the lacrosse players said. "You two need some privacy over here so you can get it on?"

"Stop," said one of the boys in the trench coats, and he pushed the lacrosse stick away roughly. Then both boys got up and walked away. They always walked away; they never fought.

We did not know if the boys in the trench coats were actually gay. We thought they were probably not—after all, their comic books featured towering, big-breasted women with eyes like Bambi's. We wondered if we should have stepped in, intervened somehow. But we decided that we were readers, not fighters, and there was nothing we could have done. Although we felt powerful in our little circle of orange chairs, we knew our authority did not extend beyond our editorial decisions. We were not the type of people who were listened to in our school. We were farther up in the social hierarchy than the boys in the black trench coats, but we were no match for the lacrosse players.

So this essay, this stunningly good essay, had been written by one of the boys in the trench coats who had just left the library. "You sure the other one didn't write an essay too?" we said. We looked through the pile. Only one boy had written an essay. "What will he do if his friend gets the position? They'll have to be apart." And then we decided that no, they couldn't be apart; the other boy in the trench coat would sit across the room and stare at us throughout our meetings. We decided it would be creepy.

We could not deny that the trench coat boy's essay was good. The story he had chosen to discuss was not written by a member of the editorial board. He skewered the story, pointed out that no conflict was ever established, the characterization was weak, and the constant alliteration was overwhelming. It was an essay that would have gotten an A from Mr. Morgan, the toughest English teacher in the school. It was really, really good, far better than the eighteen other applications. The essay made us realize our mistake in publishing the story. We were shocked; we had never heard this trench coat boy speak in any of our classes. We'd thought that maybe he was a little bit retarded because of his droopy, head-down walk and his love of comic books.

Our magazine would be ruined if we gave him a spot. Trench coat boy absolutely could not be on our staff. We'd lose our credibility. We could not be a part of a failing magazine; we had known only success in our lives. This is what we decided: he was a traitor. He did not have the right spirit for the magazine; he could not criticize what had already been published. We did not mention the fact that we asked for an in-depth analysis, and he did what was asked. We did not admit that he had written the best essay. We spent time rehashing things, making ourselves believe the other essays were better than they really were, convincing ourselves that we were making the right decision. We were glad the lacrosse players had driven the trench coat boys away; we could not look at the one who wrote the essay. We would feel too guilty if he pushed his hair out of his face and stared right at us with his tar-dark eyes.

And so we chose two new staff members, a boy and a girl, both safe, unobjectionable selections. We posted our choices in the English annex of the school. We didn't bother sending rejection letters to the people who had not been chosen. They would figure it out.

Two weeks later, the boy in the trench coat, the one who wrote the essay for us, shot himself in the school cafeteria. His friend was not there; he was home sick for the day. We cobbled together the details of the shooting. No one was paying attention; the boy was not someone who was considered important enough to notice, so everyone had a different account of the events. We were not even sure what was true and what had been changed through repeated retellings, but these were the details we heard the most: The boy sat alone. He ate his lunch, a rectangle of dry, almost burnt pizza, a serving of peas, a cup of syrupy, oversweet peach slices. It was an awful last meal. He took a small black gun out of the pocket of his trench coat. He did not wave it around. He did not make threats. He simply placed the gun in his mouth and pulled the trigger. The only detail we were sure of, the only thing we saw with our own eyes, was that blood spattered the wall behind him. We remained in the cafeteria for only a few seconds before we were ushered outside and the cafeteria doors were shut and locked, the adults tending to matters they thought were too complicated for young people to understand. We were sent home for the rest of the day.

After the shooting, school was closed for a week. There was a memorial service for the boy, but we could not bear to go. We could only bear to do one thing: talk. We talked to our classmates, to our parents, to the reporters who lingered in the school's parking lot and near the bleachers by the football field. We talked to each other at the orthodontist's office and at the DMV, waiting in line to take our driver's tests. We could not stop trying to explain what had happened. "It was a political statement, a protest against the war," we said. Or, "There were signs of trouble. If only the guidance counselors had done their jobs right, this could have been avoided." Or, "Maybe it was the lacrosse boys who caused this with their constant taunting." We talked and talked, but it didn't make us feel any better.

The next week, school reopened. There was an assembly and counselors were brought in to give presentations about the grieving process. They tried to reassure us, but no one felt reassured. They told us they would be at the school all week and we could come talk to them whenever we wanted, even during classes. They said they would write notes to our teachers so we could be let out of class. They said it was OK to be sad.

This was what we wanted to know: What did the walls of the cafeteria look like? Would we see traces of blood spatter? At lunchtime we scanned the room carefully. There was no blood. We looked from floor to ceiling—it was clean; whoever had scrubbed and painted the cafeteria had done an excellent job.

No one could eat in the freshly painted cafeteria. We told each other it was the sour paint smell. Instead of eating, we talked. We talked about anything and everything, except about the boy in the trench coat. It seemed too strange to talk about him in the place where it happened, but we needed to fill the heavy air with something, so we found other things to chatter about. We talked about helping our fathers pick leaves out of the rain gutters, we talked about what we watched on TV the night before, we talked about how we'd plan much tastier lunches if we were in charge of the cafeteria. We talked until the bell rang and it was time for us to go to our next class; we dumped our uneaten lunches into gray trash cans and left the empty, spotless cafeteria.

On Wednesday the editorial board of *Semicolon* reconvened. We sat in our squishy orange chairs and looked at the dark corner of the library. It was empty, and a fluorescent light in that section of the room flickered. The library seemed extra quiet. We told ourselves it was because none of the lacrosse players had detention. Teachers were scared to give detention; they were afraid of hurting our fragile teenage souls.

And then we saw him—the other boy in the black trench coat. We could not believe he had come back. But of course he had; what else could he do?

We watched him pass our circle of chairs, and we heard the clacking of his unlaced shoelaces against his high black boots. He did not look at us, just stared ahead as if he had someplace very important to go. He was holding a well-worn graphic novel tight to his side, his fingers curling around its softened edges. We stared at him as he wove through the ficus trees that sat in large cinnamon-colored pots in a row in the middle of the library, and waited as he made his way to the back corner under the flickering light and sat down at his usual table. We stared as he thumbed through his book front to back then back to front. He did this again and again, not stopping on any page, not reading anything. His eyes looked raw.

We had work to do, stories and poems to read and judge, but no one picked up the poem on top of our pile of papers. No one moved at all. We snuck glances at the boy, trying to be surreptitious. But it didn't matter; the boy didn't notice us in our circle of orange chairs. He looked down at the book in his hands, stared at just one page for far too long under the buzz and flicker of the fluorescent light. This was the angst, chaos, and brokenheartedness of our favorite poems and stories coming alive right in front of us, and it made us uncomfortable and sad. And finally, for once, we were speechless.

....

Late Night with Brad Mack

....

From the front row of the studio audience, Spence watches the stage. His father, talk show host Brad Mack, springs up from behind his desk, flings his tie over his left shoulder, and says, "Punch me!" He points to his stomach.

"No way, man," says Xander Marlow. He laughs, and the too-loud, too-confident laugh reminds Spence of the frat boys at his school who get drunk and break lightbulbs all over campus and guffaw as they run away from the shattered glass. Xander is the first guest on this evening's show, and he lounges casually on a purple couch, as if he were relaxing at home. Xander Marlow is nineteen, one year older than Spence. He is richer and more famous than Spence will ever be. He is the type of boy Spence is sure his father wishes he had for a son. Each of Xander's obscenely muscled biceps likely has a larger circumference than Spence's head. It is obvious that Xander spends most of his time working out. One thing is certain: Xander isn't spending his time taking acting classes. The paparazzi love taking photos of him coming out of gyms in LA in sweaty tank tops. Spence sees these photos on the celebrity gossip blogs he furtively reads on his laptop in his dorm room. He likes to leave the books from his English classes— this semester *Native Son*, *The Canterbury Tales*, *Midnight's Children*—on prominent display on his desk so that people, girls mostly, who drift into his room will think he's smart and studious, but he secretly likes scouring gossip blogs for information about his father. He has learned more about the women his father is dating and where he's been dining from these blogs than from their infrequent, stilted phone conversations.

Xander stars as Bartholomieu Beauregard, a French half-zombie half-vampire in the Zombipire movie trilogy. He is on *Late Night with Brad Mack* to promote the third movie in the trilogy, *Zombipire on Fire*. Although Spence is aware that a zombie and a vampire could not—should not—breed, he thinks that if they somehow did, their offspring would not be tanned and bulging with muscles. A zombipire—if the thing existed at all—would be skinny, pale, and scared of sunlight. There should be a sense of death and a whiff of rot associated with a zombipire.

"I can take it!" Spence's father yells. "Look at these abs." He untucks his dress shirt and lifts it to reveal his tanned, chiseled stomach. The tan is fake, orangish. Spence is mortified. His father is fifty-one years old, old enough to know that he should keep his clothes on during a talk show interview.

"Punch him!" the audience shouts. They must think this is a gag, something planned.

Xander stares vacantly at the camera. Spence can tell that this wasn't scripted. Nothing on the pale blue index cards that are now scattered on Spence's father's desk says anything about a punch. The notecards contain prompts to help Spence's father steer the conversation, but they are off script, and Spence realizes Xander is not smart enough to know what to do. He notes the blankness in Xander's eyes; perhaps the casting agent was onto something, after all, when choosing him to be part zombie.

"Come on!" says Spence's father.

His father is acting like an imbecile, and Spence knows that this sort of idiocy is why his father is in last place in the late night ratings. This is why he will never be moved out of the 1:35 a.m. slot, why the show is always on the verge of cancellation. Spence knows people only watch because they're waiting for Brad Mack to do something ridiculous and stupid. This punching dare might have been funny if it were more incongruous, if that host with the birdlike tuft of gray hair and the potbelly asked Xander to hit him. Or if the host who'd just had the quadruple bypass demanded a punch. It'd be an admission that Xander is young and strong and the host is aging, and Xander would know what to do: he'd punch lightly, and the host would fall over, pretend that Xander knocked him out. Then maybe the host would hold up Xander's arm as if he were the winner of a boxing match and demand that Xander flex one of his enormous muscles. But in this case it's embarrassing. Spence's father is actually trying to prove he's young and fit and virile, just like Xander Marlow. And even dumb and possibly roided-up Xander has the sense to know that punching Brad Mack will come to no good. Spence's father shouts, "You won't hurt me! I have abs of steel!"

So Xander stands up, makes a loose fist, and punches Spence's father. It's a light punch, no windup. Spence's father says, "I couldn't even feel that! Are you a little girl?"

"What?" says Xander, confused. Spence is certain no one has ever made fun of Xander to his face before. If you are big and handsome and possess a modicum of charm, people are nice to you. Xander says, "No, I'm not a girl." He looks down at his body, as if examining it for confirmation.

"See," says Spence's father, turning to the audience, "this is the problem with gym muscles. They look pumped up, but I bet you can hardly lift a gallon of water without breaking a sweat."

Now Xander's look of confusion is replaced by anger. Someone smarter would laugh off the comments, knowing that the next day in the gossip blogs Brad Mack will seem like a jackass and people will speculate about whether he's back on painkillers. But Xander will not just sit there and be insulted on national television. He shrugs off his blazer, and the crowd hoots—they must still think this is a rehearsed skit—and he pulls his right arm back and slams his fist into the middle of Spence's father's stomach. Spence bolts up straight to see his father's reaction, but nothing happens for a few seconds, as if Spence is watching this on TV and someone has pressed Pause. There is silence in the studio, the audience in a breathless hush, the band gripping their instruments tightly so as not to let a stray strum or tap escape. Spence's father grins widely at the camera, about to say something he probably thinks is clever or hilarious, but before the words can come out, he falls backward and onto the floor.

At the hospital, Spence sits in the waiting room next to Harvey Kim, the announcer for *Late Night with Brad Mack*. There are a handful of other people in the waiting room, none of whom looks particularly upset or worried. A middle-aged woman is perched on the edge of a table next to a pile of magazines and flips through an old issue of *Us Weekly*. A teenage boy wearing enormous headphones bobs his head in time to music Spence cannot hear, and across from him a white-haired man works through a book of crossword puzzles. In the corner, a mother reads a book to her toddler, whose eyelids are growing heavy.

Harvey is the one who drove Spence to the hospital. An ambulance brought Spence's father. The show for this evening has been cancelled, and Harvey has already gotten a call on his cell phone to tell him the network has decided to air reruns for the rest of the week. After that, they'll see how Spence's father is doing. Spence wonders whether this might be the opportunity the network heads have been hoping for to cancel *Late Night with Brad Mack*.

"You don't have to wait," Spence says.

"I'll hang around," Harvey says. "Your father, he'll be OK. Likely just had the wind knocked out of him."

This probably isn't true. The studio's doctor examined Spence's father and determined he needed to go to the hospital to be checked for internal bleeding. He also has a cut and bump on the back of his head from the fall. He's getting stitches now. But Spence isn't worried. His father is a lucky man; things always work out for him.

Spence is just visiting his father for spring break; he's flown across the country from Ohio, where he goes to college. He was supposed to go on a spring break trip with his friend Kirby, whom he's known almost all his life. Kirby goes to Amherst, and he and Spence were planning to meet in New York City to have an adventure. Spence has a long essay due in a few weeks for his memoir writing class, and he wanted to take the trip to New York so he could have something interesting to write about.

He could write essays for class about his father, but no one in Ohio knows he's Brad Mack's son. Spence doesn't want anyone to know. People always think he's more interesting when they find out who his father is, but that feels unfair. If he were willing, though, he'd have plenty to write about his father, about the stupid, reckless things he would do when he was upset, about the crazy ways he'd spend money when he was flush with cash. Spence could write about the hot air balloon his father bought after his first show aired. He'd paid four stagehands to haul it to their backyard, then left it there for seven months because he had no idea how to fly it. Spence could write about the guilt he feels now because his father—to whom he rarely speaks—is paying for his college education, fifty-seven thousand dollars a year for a private college when he could have gone to a state university nearly for free since his mother is a reference librarian at UCSD. He could write about how angry he was when he found out his mother didn't ask for spousal support from his father when they'd divorced. All she wanted was to keep the small house in San Diego and for Spence's father to support his son financially. Spence wasn't supposed to know these things, but he'd overheard his grandmother telling his mother that it was idiotic of her, after all those years of putting up with Spence's father, to ask for so little. But if he hadn't overheard this, he would have still figured it out. His mother lives in the same modest house he lived in as a kid, she drives an eleven-year-old Toyota, she buys her clothes at T. J. Maxx.

Spence could write about those early years his father spent as a salesman in the ladies' shoe department of Neiman Marcus, how he was able to charm woman after woman into buying expensive shoes and how every month he was always the salesman with the highest commission. And Spence could write about how every few months his father would bring home a pair for Spence's mother, one shoe worn and creased, the floor sample that hundreds of women had held and touched, and the other shoe perfectly new. These shoes delighted his mother, and even then, as a small boy, Spence thought she shouldn't have been so happy with so little. He could write about how his mother still wears some of these shoes all these years later, now both sides looking equally worn and scuffed, and when he asks her why she doesn't just throw them away, she tells him it's foolish to get rid of shoes that are still wearable. But he will not write about these things for his class; these are not things anyone needs to know about, these are private things.

Because he doesn't want to write about his father, he needs to have adventures to write about. And this is why he needed to go to New York, but Kirby called a few days before their trip was supposed to start and said he had too much work to do and would flunk out of school if he didn't get it all done over spring break. He'd have to bail on the trip. Spence knew that Kirby's idea of flunking was getting a B+. He tried to convince Kirby that he desperately needed this trip, but Kirby said, "Maybe another time, man." So that spring break plan was out, and Spence called his mother and told her he'd come home to stay with her in San Diego. But she reminded him that she already had plans for the week; she was going to Paris with two of the women who worked with her at the library. She'd told him about this trip when he was home for winter break, but he'd brushed it off, thought it would never come to be because his mother never went anywhere. But the tickets were now purchased and she was going. "I could just stay at school over break," he said, although he didn't really want to. The only people who would be around would be the international students, and they only hung out with other people from their countries of origin. "We'll figure something out," his mother said before she hung up the phone.

An hour later, she called back and said, "Your father said you can stay with him over spring break. I just got off the phone with him." Spence insisted he could stay alone at his mother's house, but she said it would be good for him to spend time with his father.

After all these years, his mother still thinks it's best for Spence to have a relationship with his father, even though Spence has explained to her that sometimes people who are cut from different cloth just can't see eye to eye. "You are fifty percent your father's cloth," she'd said. "That doesn't even make sense," Spence said. But Spence likes the metaphor of people as cloth. His mother would be something practical and durable, clean white cotton, freshly ironed. His father would be something garish and gaudy, the clingy polyester of a cheap Halloween costume from Walmart with hems that unravel during the first wearing. How had these two people—so enormously different—seen each other for the first time in their discussion section for Introductory French in college and decided they belonged together? Even back then, hadn't it been obvious how different they were?

Spence hears the sound of change jingling in a pocket and looks up and sees Harvey standing over him. "You want a soda?" Harvey says.

Spence shakes his head, and Harvey goes off to find the vending machines. Spence has an incredible fondness for Harvey. He's known him for nine years; they met right before the first episode of *Late Night with Brad Mack* aired. This was back when his parents were still together, and the fact that his father was becoming successful was exciting to Spence. It felt important that his father had his own announcer, that Harvey was on the show to say his father's name and list who the guests were each night. His father had introduced Spence to many people in show business, and Harvey was the only one who remembered his name and how old he was. Spence had liked Harvey from the first time they'd met: he had a deep, booming voice, but he was tiny, maybe five-one or five-two, so he wasn't scary the way a huge man with a big voice would be.

When Spence was eleven, he'd discovered that Harvey was the voice of Inspector Nestor, the lemur on Spence's favorite animated children's program, *Blue Zoo Crew*. Harvey had never mentioned his voiceover work, but one day, while his parents were going through their divorce, Spence indulged in a *Blue Zoo Crew* marathon, even though he was too old to be watching it. He knew it was a stupid show—

it was about a group of blue cartoon animals that escaped the zoo each night to solve crimes—but it reminded him of when he was a little kid and spent happy Saturday mornings watching it. During the third episode of his viewing marathon, he'd noticed that the lemur's voice sounded familiar, and he'd waited for the credits, and there was Harvey's name. The next time Spence saw Harvey, he asked, "What's it like being Inspector Nestor?" and Harvey said, "It's like every other job: you show up, do your work, get a paycheck. Mostly I recorded lines alone in a sound booth." Spence wanted more. He was used to listening to his father's boasts and tales of rubbing elbows with famous people. Spence didn't know what to do when Harvey acted as if it was no big deal that he was Inspector Nestor's voice. Back then—back when Spence had been so impressed by the talk show and the famous friends—it was easy talking with his father. He just had to listen and say "That's cool" when his father told his stories, but what should you say when someone told you that something they did was no big deal?

By the time Spence was in high school, he'd found something else to admire about Harvey: he was a sharp dresser. By fourteen, Spence realized that he would not be tall, that he'd inherited the shortness gene from his mother. He observed little men closely: his biology teacher, his dentist, the man at the pet store who sold Spence food for his canary. They all wore clothes that were too big, polo shirts whose sleeves hung to their elbows, pants that sagged in the rear. Dr. Goldstein's dentist coat was at least three sizes too large, making him look like a child pretending to be a dentist. Mr. Slattery, Spence's biology teacher, always wore belts that looped one and a half times around and tucked pathetically into a back belt loop. Then there was Harvey, with his perfectly tailored shirts, his pants that never needed to be rolled up at the cuffs. And Harvey's wife was beautiful and friendly, a lawyer who worked to protect the environment—and all of it, the clothes and the wife and the announcing and voiceover skills, gave Spence hope that although he would not grow to be a big and popular guy like his father, his life could be OK.

"Here," Harvey says, handing Spence a root beer.

"Oh," says Spence. "Thank you." Does Harvey know that root beer is his favorite kind of soda? Has he told him this? Most vending machines don't have root beer. Maybe Harvey sought out the root beer for him, maybe he even left the hospital and drove to a convenience store to find it. Spence stares at the bottle in his hand and thinks Harvey knows him better than his own father does.

"You don't have to drink it now," Harvey says. "I just thought you might get thirsty."

"Yeah, definitely. This is great, fantastic. Thank you, Harvey. So much."

"It's just a soda," Harvey says.

"Did you remember that I like root beer best?" Spence says.

"I pressed the Coke button and this came out instead."

"Oh," says Spence. This revelation is crushing.

Harvey twists the top off his 7UP and takes a long swig. "Your father said you're quite the poet. You got something published?"

How does his father know this? His mother must have bragged when they'd spoken on the phone.

"It was no big deal. The journal was only open to freshmen at my school, and they were desperate for submissions."

"No one will know that if you don't tell them."

"Yeah, well. It's the truth." Spence opens his root beer and it bubbles and overflows. He has no napkins, so he just lets the soda dribble onto the floor.

"Come on," orders a sharp female voice, and Spence looks up from the pooling root beer by his feet. A woman with hair dyed bright orange storms into the waiting room with Xander Marlow. She tugs on the sleeve of his leather jacket. The woman is dressed nicely, in a skirt and high heels and a silky green blouse, but her hair is a tangled mess. Xander cradles a motorcycle helmet under one arm. The nurses and the other people in the waiting room stare at him.

"I don't know—" Xander begins.

"You *have* to talk to him," the woman says. She charges up to the nurses' station and demands to see Brad Mack.

"The doctor is still with him," says a nurse wearing purple scrubs.

"I don't think you understand. I need to talk to him ASAP," the red-headed woman says. She is agitated, her hands curled into fists, and Spence wonders if she's going to pummel the nurse.

"I think I should leave," Xander says. People are still watching him, fascinated, as if he's the star of a play set in a hospital waiting room. The boy with the giant headphones takes a picture of Xander on his cell phone.

"You stay. Sit," the redheaded woman says to Xander. She speaks to him as if he is a golden retriever, and Xander obediently lowers himself into a beige plastic seat across from Spence.

Harvey says, "Meghan. Wait with us. He's getting stitches now."

"Oh," she says. "I didn't even see you." Spence doesn't like the way she says it, as if she didn't see Harvey because he is too tiny, a speck of nothingness.

"Have you met Spence yet?" Harvey says. "Spence is Brad's son."

"*You're* Spence?" Meghan says, looking him up and down.

He doesn't like the way she says this either, as if he is just as un-important as miniature, invisible Harvey, as if there's no way he can be biologically related to his father. He stares at her. He's seen photos of her coming out of some fancy sushi restaurant with his father, but in those photos her hair was smooth, shiny. She is his father's newest girlfriend and is apparently a social media strategist, which sounds like one of those nothing jobs made to sound important. Spence is pretty sure Meghan writes most of his father's Facebook status updates and pretends to be him on Twitter; all of it always seems far too chipper to have actually come from his father.

"What's wrong?" Meghan says. "It's my hair, isn't it?" She brings her hands to her head. Her fingers are stuck in the tangles, and Spence hears crunchy hair-ripping noises as she extricates them.

"It's a little windblown," Harvey says.

"I was near the studio when I saw what happened on Twitter. So I ran over and needed a ride to the hospital. I came on the back of Xander's motorcycle. He didn't have an extra helmet."

Spence and Harvey look at Xander, who blushes. "I'm sorry," he says, "but I signed a contract saying I have to wear a helmet when I ride. To protect my brain."

Meghan sighs. "How bad is my hair?"

"Your hair is fine," Harvey says. "Perhaps the concern here should be about Brad."

"I *am* concerned," Meghan says. "That's why I'm here."

Spence stares at Meghan, trying to figure out how old she is and whether it's appropriate for his father to date her. She has little wrinkles around her eyes, but her face looks young. But he can't make a final judgment about her age because the crazy hair is too distracting.

"Please stop looking at me like that," she says. "I don't appreciate the male gaze upon me like that."

"What? I wasn't . . ." He feels as if he's involved in one of the inane conversations he always seems to get into at school with girls he can't bring himself to be normal around because they are too smart or too beautiful or too intimidating. But Meghan is none of these things.

"What were you looking at?" Meghan demands.

"I just wanted to figure out whether you were closer in age to me or my father," Spence says, and Meghan looks hard at him for a moment and collapses into a chair.

"Oh, God," she says. "How old are you?"

"Eighteen. My father is fifty-one."

"I *know* that," she says. "I am very much aware."

Xander stands and says, "Since he can't have visitors, maybe I can send him balloons tomorrow. I need to get to my Krav Maga class."

"No, you need to talk to him and resolve this matter," Meghan says. "Sit down."

Xander plants himself back in his seat. Spence catches him staring at his own reflection in the mirrory black of his motorcycle helmet.

Meghan reaches into a giant purse on her lap, pulls out a gift-wrapped book, and hands it to Spence. "Your dad asked me to pick this up for you. It's a present from him. I've been hauling it around all day."

Spence sets his root beer bottle on the floor, wipes his hands on his jeans, and takes the gift. The wrapping is dark green, and there's a gold sticker on it that says Barnes & Noble. He sighs.

"What? Do you not know how to read?" Meghan says.

"Meghan," says Harvey. "Please." He sounds like he's her father.

"What?" she says. "I bust my ass to get this book, I carry it around all day, and then the kid sighs like I've just handed him a dog turd."

"Language, please," says Harvey.

Spence says, "I was just sighing because of Barnes & Noble. With all of my father's money, I'd think he'd support independent bookstores."

Meghan snorts. "Don't be so certain your father is rolling in dough."

"Are you going to open it?" Xander says.

Spence looks up and sees that Xander Marlow is still there. How had he forgotten that Xander, in all his bigness and famousness, is still sitting there?

Spence puts a finger under one flap of wrapping paper and rips the paper down the center of the book. It is *The Poetry of Robert Frost*. Of course his father would buy him Frost poems. Robert Frost is the poet that people who don't know anything about poetry know about.

"Why are you sighing again?" Meghan says.

"You wouldn't get it," Spence says. But there's an indignity to it all, his father's snippy girlfriend presenting him with a book of Frost poems purchased from a large, soulless corporation.

"You're an ingrate," Meghan says.

"I'm grateful you carried this book in your supersized purse all day, OK?" Spence says.

"You guys sound like brother and sister," Xander says, and Spence and Meghan look at each other, both clearly appalled.

No one says anything for a few seconds, then Meghan says, "I'm way too old to be his sister."

"How old *are* you?" says Spence.

"Twenty-eight."

They *could* be siblings; the math would work out.

"Can I see the book?" Xander says.

"You want to see it? Or read it?" Spence says.

"I love Robert Frost," Xander says.

"*You* like poetry?" says Meghan. Spence waits for her to ask Xander whether he can read, but she does not.

Spence hands Xander the book, and Xander says, "When I was in school I wasn't so great at English, but we did this poetry unit in tenth grade, and we read some of these poems, and they were, like, not boring."

"A ringing endorsement," Meghan says.

"Meghan," Harvey says, once again sounding like he's her father.

"I'm sorry," Meghan says. "I'm just stressed about Bradley."

Xander flips through the book and stops. "This one," he says, "'Home Burial.'" He reads the poem silently, a finger tracing the words, his mouth moving as he reads. Spence will not allow himself to glance at Meghan. He knows she will look snotty and disapproving. But Spence does not want to mock Xander Marlow right now, even though he generally has contempt for people who mouth words when they read.

"That's one of his most famous poems," Spence says.

"That's true," says Meghan. "I was an English major in college."

"Famous things aren't bad," Xander says. "Sometimes things get famous because they're good."

Spence wants to say that famous things, overexposed things, including Xander himself, are, in many cases, bad. But instead he says, "Why do you like that poem so much?"

"It made me sad. Like this couple and their dead baby. And I got what he was saying, you know? Up to that point in school I never felt anything, ever, from anything I read. Then I was reading this poem and feeling really sad, and it was kind of like, 'Whoa.' You know what I mean?"

Perhaps it is not the most eloquent defense of poetry Spence has ever heard, but he understands. After all, doesn't he want to write poems to make readers feel something? When Spence's poem came out in the literary journal, he showed it to his roommate, Ted, a perpetually sunburned boy from Youngstown whose sole purpose at the college, it seemed, was to play soccer.

"Did you get paid?" Ted said, not looking away from *Grand Theft Auto* on his computer.

"No, of course not."

"Why would you let them publish your poem if they didn't give you money?" Ted said.

"It's not how things work. Do you want to read it?"

"Maybe later. Put it over there," Ted said, gesturing to a pile of books he'd purchased in the college's bookstore during the first week of the semester and had not cracked open yet. It was frustrating; no one at school understood what it meant to write a poem and want someone to be affected by it.

"It was nice of your dad to get you this," Xander says.

"It's just a book," Spence says.

"Don't you like books?"

"I guess."

"My dad's never bought me a book. He wants me to buy him a car. An Escalade."

"When you get famous, people want stuff from you," Meghan says, as if she knows what it's like to be famous.

"Yeah," says Xander. "People you never knew existed try to convince you that they're your cousins or something so you'll buy them things."

He sounds so sad, and Spence feels a bubble of niceness rising in his chest. Usually he tries to suppress his urges toward kindness, but now he feels so sorry for Xander that he wants to give him the Frost book, which feels like a very strange thing to want to do. But before Spence can say anything, a nurse comes into the waiting room and heads toward their small group. "Oh my god," she says. "Xander Marlow. In my waiting room." She pauses, then says, "Are any of you family?" She looks hopefully at Xander, who shakes his head.

Spence says, "I'm his son."

"I'm practically family," Meghan says, and Harvey says, "No, you're not."

"You can follow me," says the nurse, pointing to Spence. "You're definitely not related?" she asks Xander. He shakes his head again.

Spence wonders which of them his father would most want to see. Harvey? Meghan? Probably his dad would most like a visit from tall, handsome, famous, successful Xander Marlow, who apparently also loves Robert Frost.

"You need to promise not to sue," Meghan says, moving to sit in the seat Spence has just vacated.

"I was the one who punched him," Xander says.

"But it could be argued that it was provoked," says Meghan.

"Can I leave if I promise I won't sue?"

"First we should get a photo of you two together, maybe like you leaning over his hospital bed, both of you smiling, with your thumbs up. We can tweet that photo to all of Bradley's fans."

"That sounds totally lame and cheesy," Xander says, and as Spence follows the nurse down the hallway, he thinks maybe Xander is not that dumb after all.

"Your son's here to see you, Mr. Mack," the nurse says.

"Call me Brad, please. After all you've done for me, I can't have you calling me Mr. Mack." His voice sounds creaky, dry.

"OK, Brad," the nurse says.

"That's better," says Spence's father. "Ellen, Spence. Spence, Ellen. Ellen is the best nurse in the world."

Ellen grins at Spence's father, and Spence can tell she's happy with the compliment. Spence doesn't know what to do. Should he shake the nurse's hand? She's already walked him in from the waiting room, so it's not like they're just meeting for the first time. His father always knows what to do and say to make people feel good; Spence does not.

But his own awkwardness is at least genuine, real, and his father, as charming as he can be, is disingenuous, always on a mission to make as many people like him as possible.

"Take it easy on him," Ellen says to Spence. "You can only stay for a few minutes, and then he'll need to rest." She walks out of the room and leaves the two of them alone.

"My boy," Spence's father says. "Just the person I wanted to see."

"Harvey drove me here."

"Is he still here?"

Spence nods, and his father looks pleased. He sits up, and Spence can see a large piece of gauze taped to his scalp.

"Harvey's a good guy. Every man needs a Harvey in his life. You have a Harvey?"

"Maybe." He thinks about Kirby, who bailed on their spring break trip. "No, I don't think so."

"You're young still. You'll find your Harvey."

"Where's your hair?" Spence says. His father's entire head has been shaved. He looks like a fuzzy newborn animal.

"I asked them to shave it all off. They'd just shaved off a patch so I could get stiches, but that looked funny."

The stubble on his father's head is white. Has he been dyeing his hair? His father coughs, and Spence sees pain wash over his face.

"Are you OK?" Spence says.

"It's nothing. You know how doctors are. Too cautious."

"Can I see your stomach?" Spence says.

"There's really nothing to see."

"Please?" He feels like a child, but he wants to know if his father is lying; he wants to try to gauge how much pain he is actually in.

Spence's father pulls down the blanket then lifts the edge of his hospital gown. "I haven't looked at it yet," he says. "But I'm sure it's nothing." He does not look at his own stomach and instead focuses his eyes on the ceiling.

It's not nothing. It's mottled gray and purple and red and looks swollen and painful. "My god," Spence says. "What did the doctor say?"

"Oh, this stomach has seen worse." Spence's father attempts to laugh, but only a coughy, brittle sound comes out. His face crinkles in pain. Spence wonders if his father has refused painkillers. He's not supposed to take them anymore. Five years ago, he crashed his Ferrari into his garage very late one night. Afterward he said his back hurt—Spence is still unsure whether his father was really in pain, because he was walking just fine—and doctor after doctor prescribed him too many painkillers.

"I'm sorry about this," Spence's father says. He pulls his hospital gown back over his stomach. "I ruined our week."

"You didn't punch yourself. Xander Marlow punched you. He's in the waiting room. Meghan's here too. She wants him to promise not to sue you."

"Good. The last thing I need is a lawsuit."

"Why'd you dare Xander to punch you?"

Spence's father pauses then says, "Because you were there."

"Yeah, but so were two hundred other people." Spence thinks his father is blaming him, saying his presence somehow caused all of this. He wants to defend himself.

"Yes, but you, you were right there. In the front row watching me."

Is his father telling him that he was performing for him? Before his father got his show, they would play talk show at home, and Spence always had to be the audience. Once, early on, he'd asked his father if he could be the host, but his father said no. Then he'd asked if he could be the bandleader, but his father looked at him holding his viola and said he didn't think any bandleaders had ever, in all of history, played viola. His father wouldn't even let him pretend to be a guest. That job was reserved for Winston, their old, grumpy bulldog who lazily slumped in a chair next to Spence's father. His father would pretend Winston was a rock star or a politician or a movie star and would ask probing questions and Winston would either drool, snort, or fall asleep and snore in response. Spence found all of this hysterical and sat laughing in his small wooden chair on which his father had painted "V.I.P. Audience Seating." By the time he was eight, Spence grew tired of playing talk show and began to resent the fact that his sole job was to cheer his father on. But now he thinks that maybe he misunderstood. Maybe it was important to his father to impress Spence, to make him laugh.

"Hey, what do you think of Meghan?" his father asks.

Spence wants to tell his father that Meghan is terrible, awful, obnoxious, but instead turns to the word everyone uses in his literature classes to talk about readings they don't like. "I think she's problematic," he says.

"She's Harvey's niece. She's not my girlfriend."

"But I've seen pictures—"

"She got her MBA and then the economy tanked. She was trying to sell herself as an image consultant and a social media strategist, but no one would hire her. So I hired her. And then people kept taking pictures of our meetings and assuming we were together, and she said maybe it wouldn't be a bad idea for people to think I was dating a businesswoman and not another actress."

Although Spence doesn't think businesswoman is exactly the right term to describe Meghan, it occurs to him that this might be the nicest thing his father has ever done, that his father is actually capable of kindness. For so long he has only thought of his father as an insincere showman, flashy and full of tricks, but what if there is more to him? This is not something Spence has considered before.

"Did Meghan remember to give you something?"

"The book?"

"Meghan wanted to get you an iTunes gift card, but I told her you'd like the book more. I bet you're a big Robert Frost fan, right?"

"I guess. Thanks." His father looks weak, vulnerable, and Spence does not think this is the right time to debate the merits of Frost's poetry. "So Meghan's your employee, right?"

"Technically, but mostly she bosses me around. Harvey said she's always been bossy, even when she was a baby. He and his sister, Meghan's mom, used to call her the little dictator. It's like a very bad marriage, what Meghan and I have. She tells me what to do. I do the exact opposite. With your mother and me, it was nothing like that. That fell apart because of me. None of that was your mother's fault."

He doesn't sound like himself, has never spoken to Spence this way before. Spence is worried that something is terribly wrong. "Why are you talking like this? Are you dying?"

Spence's father tries laughing again, and this time a rough-edged laugh comes out. "I'm not dying, Spence. But maybe the pain is making me talkative."

"I thought you weren't in pain."

"You got me," Spence's father says, and then Spence knows that he truly hurts. He wouldn't normally back down so easily. "Hey, your mom read me that poem you wrote. It was fantastic."

"It's nothing," Spence says. He's embarrassed about the poem now. It was about a beach vacation he'd taken with his parents when he was six years old. This was back when his father was not famous. Back then he'd disappear for hours most nights after working a full day selling shoes. On those nights, he went to comedy clubs to perform, and then Spence would wake up when he heard his father's car in the driveway, and he would eavesdrop on the conversations in his parents' bedroom next door. Each night his father said hardly anyone showed up or the crowd didn't laugh at his jokes. And each night Spence's mother said he had to keep going if this was something he really wanted. His father was around so rarely then, and his mother had been in graduate school for library science and spent most of her time studying. But this trip to the beach stuck out in Spence's mind because his parents had paid so much attention to him all weekend.

In the poem, which he'd titled "Meal Fit for a King," he'd written about how much he'd loved the picnic lunch his mother had packed— grapes and egg salad sandwiches she'd kept cold with blue frozen ice packs, and Oreos that had ended up cold, too—and how the food tasted better on the beach than it ever had at home. The poem began: "On the blanket I could look and see / up to my father/ literally and metaphorically." His Introduction to Poetry professor seemed genuinely furious and offended by that beginning and told him, "It is imperative that those lines be expunged." The poem ended: "It was a meal fit for a king / and my father/ was my king / and the beach his golden kingdom." His professor had called the poem sentimental and over-wrought, and Spence had submitted it to the literary journal only to spite her, to show her it was publishable, but now he wishes he'd never done it. She was right, of course, the poem overflowing with emotions Spence does not want to admit he ever felt.

"It was the best poem I ever read," says Spence's father, and it feels so strange to have this attention focused on him, and now Spence understands Harvey's modest reaction when he'd wanted to talk about Inspector Nestor.

"It's a kind of problematic poem," Spence says.

"It was perfect," says his father, and Spence thinks about how his professor told his class to never trust anyone who claimed your writing was perfect. But this feels good, nice, to have someone who understands what he was trying to communicate in his poem, no matter how overwrought it was. "I'd forgotten about that day and then your mother read me the poem and it came flooding back. You even remembered the Oreos."

"I don't know if I got all the details right."

His father waves a hand and says, "Details don't matter!"

Spence thinks about his poetry professor again, how she always said details mattered the most.

"Do you think I could get a copy of the poem? I want to frame it and hang it up."

"Are you sure you're not dying?" Spence says, and Ellen, the nurse, reappears and says, "He'll be fine. Just bruised and battered, but give him a month and he'll be good as new."

"I'll be up and running in a week, tops," Spence's father says.

"I'm sure that if anyone can have a miraculous recovery, it's you, Brad." She turns to Spence and tells him it's time for his father to rest.

"Call your mother," Spence's father says. "Please. Tell her I'm OK. And ask her to send me a copy of that book you wrote."

"I didn't write a book. It's a literary journal for freshmen and it's just one poem."

"Still, though, it really was the best poem I ever read."

"All right," Ellen says. "Time to go. You two can talk more about poetry later."

Back in the waiting room, Meghan is tapping rapidly on her iPhone, and Spence wonders if she's updating his father's Twitter account, filling it with cheerful, exuberant lies. She doesn't look up or acknowledge his return. The toddler across the room has woken up, and Harvey is crouched next to the child, his hand in a fluffy rabbit puppet. In a funny voice, he says, "Where are my carrots?" The toddler giggles and reaches for the rabbit's ears.

Harvey turns around and says, "Is he OK?"

"Yeah," says Spence. "He's OK."

Xander Marlow is gone. Spence looks to see if there is any evidence that Xander is coming back, but nothing belonging to him remains in the waiting room. He has taken his leather jacket and shiny helmet. When Spence gets closer to the seats, he sees that Xander has left the book of Frost's poems, and he is glad it's still there. The book rests on top of the green Barnes & Noble wrapping paper, which someone has neatly folded into a rectangle, as if frugally saving it to wrap another gift. Spence sits down. He picks up the book of poems his father wants him to have, opens it, and begins to read.

Prized Possessions

Lydia Wong grew impatient after waiting forty-five minutes for the screening of her daughter's movie to begin. While she waited, she'd noticed how many things were wrong that evening: the screening was held in a cramped art gallery, the audience had to sit on uncomfortable metal folding chairs, the room reeked of cologne, and the movie was titled *Mother of Annoyances*. In an interview with the *Post-Gazette*, Lydia's daughter, whom they'd called "young filmmaking phenom Anna Wong," had said the movie was semiautobiographical. Lydia was not looking forward to seeing the portrayal of the mother in the film.

"Ma," Anna said, approaching Lydia's chair, "I could get someone to take you home if you're tired. It's OK if you miss the screening."

"Don't be silly," Lydia said. "I'm staying. But I would rather watch a panda movie."

Anna was known for her nature documentaries. She'd traveled the world and had filmed turtles on the Galapagos Islands, elephants in Africa, and polar bears in the Arctic. Lydia kept telling Anna that her next movie should be about pandas in China, but Anna said if she did a panda movie after the polar bear one, then she'd probably be expected to do one about grizzlies after that. She didn't want to be known only for bear documentaries. This was just an excuse, thought Lydia. The problem was that Anna had no desire to travel to China, even though she should go and learn about her own heritage.

"I told you," Anna said. "I just wanted to make up a story."

"Everyone loves pandas. People stand for hours in line at the zoo in Washington, D.C., to see them," Lydia said.

"That's only when the babies are born," Anna said. "People go nuts for baby animals. Look, are you sure you don't want to leave? You're probably too hot under these lights." Anna pointed to the ceiling.

"I'm fine," Lydia said. "You go start the movie. People will leave if you don't hurry up."

Anna sighed. "Fine," she said, then she moved across the room and joined a group of young people who were drinking wine out of plastic glasses and eating small pieces of cheese speared on toothpicks. Lydia had walked by the cheese tray earlier; it smelled like stinky feet, but this didn't deter all these people from eating cube after cube as if they hadn't been fed in days.

Lydia shifted in her chair and saw her grandchildren, Chance and Hope, running up and down the narrow room like jackrabbits.

"Calm down!" shouted Lydia's son-in-law, Gray. "You two said you would act like adults tonight."

Adults! thought Lydia. Her grandchildren, twins, were ten years old, hardly adults.

"Look at these awesome photos," Gray said to Lydia, pushing his floppy blond hair out of his eyes and pointing to a wall. Lydia often thought about taking the sharp scissors she used for cutting up whole raw chickens and trimming Gray's hair. She imagined the sound of the dry hair cutting and thought those snips would be immensely satisfying.

"Maybe if your hair was out of your eyes you could see better. These photos are terrible," Lydia said. The walls were covered with black-and-white photographs of salt and pepper shakers taken at diners all over Pittsburgh. Half of the photos were blurry.

"To each his own, I guess," Gray said. "I like them."

"You would," Lydia snapped. Gray was an artist himself, *a glass artist*. This meant he sold oddly shaped vases that no flower could actually survive in to artsy stores and spent his weekends teaching people glassblowing at the Art Center. This was not the type of job a real man had. It was lucky that Anna made enough money teaching filmmaking classes to support the family.

"Why don't you go ask Anna why the movie hasn't started yet," Lydia said. Even though Anna didn't ever listen to her, she might listen to Gray. Gray walked across the room toward Anna, and Lydia watched as he moved through the crowd. No one was dressed in a respectable way, like Lydia, in her gray wool suit and stockings and her jade necklace, which had been passed down through generations of women in her family. The people at the screening were just like Anna, all wearing glasses with small rectangular frames and head-to-toe black clothing.

Lydia felt a tap on her shoulder and turned in her chair. Mimi Liu stood behind Lydia, holding a large black purse in one hand and a blue plastic bag from the supermarket in the other. She wore a bright red dress covered in yellow flowers.

"Hello!" Mimi said.

Lydia felt dizzy and thought she might slide off her chair and land flat on her back on the floor. "What are you doing here?"

Mimi scampered around to the seat next to Lydia and sat down. "I see in paper that Anna have movie here. And I see movie is free, so why not?"

Lydia knew Mimi hoped the movie would be terrible. Lydia disliked Mimi, although everyone else seemed to think they should be friends because they were almost the same age, they both lived with their children, they attended the same church, and they were both originally from Shanghai. It was ridiculous, Lydia thought, that just because people were similar in some ways they were expected to like one another. Even though they were not friends, they always seemed to be thrown together—on Sundays at church, on Wednesday evenings at choir practice—and they often bumped into each other at the only Asian grocery store in their neighborhood on Tuesday afternoons, when fresh fish arrived from New York.

"These chairs," Mimi said, wiggling, "not very comfortable. Why not show movie in theater like *real* movie?"

"This isn't a stupid car chase and explosion movie. When a movie is art they show it in a place like this," Lydia snapped. Even if she didn't approve of Anna's choice to not make a panda movie, she was still going to defend her daughter. Lydia was the only person who was allowed to criticize Anna.

They were quiet for a few moments, the only two people sitting and staring straight ahead at the screen. When it became apparent that the movie was not going to begin, Mimi picked up her plastic shopping bag. "I went to garage sale today." She withdrew a ceramic statue of Jesus from the bag. It was about six inches tall, and Jesus's hands were extended with the palms up. The folds of his robe were well rendered, and Lydia could even see the painted-in grains of leather in his brown sandals. It was a nice figurine, and Lydia could imagine it on the dresser in her bedroom.

"Guess how much I pay for Jesus," Mimi said.

"Twenty cents?" said Lydia. She knew Mimi would be upset if she grossly underestimated the price.

"No! Two dollar! But I think Jesus is valuable. One time I see Jesus just like this in museum."

"I saw a Jesus just like that in the dollar store last week," Lydia said. It was a lie, but she wanted to make Mimi feel stupid.

"You have bad eye," Mimi said in a tone that indicated she was certain she was right and Lydia was wrong.

The lights dimmed until there was only one light shining on a podium up front. Mimi put the Jesus figurine back into the plastic bag and put the bag into her purse. She slid the purse under her chair. Anna walked up to the podium. She thanked everyone for coming and supporting her. This was a small premiere, she explained, but she hoped good things might happen with the movie and that one day it would be shown in theaters across the country.

"So she *want* movie in real theaters," Mimi whispered.

Lydia did not respond. She suspected Mimi saw her as an invader in the neighborhood and wanted to drive her away. The February after Lydia moved to Pittsburgh, Anna had arranged for Lydia to give a pre-

sentation about Chinese New Year at the library. Since that presenta-
tion Mimi had been cold to Lydia, acted as if she'd taken something
away from her. Ever since Mimi had found out that Lydia's daughter
was a filmmaker, she'd given Lydia a hard time about it. Mimi would
boast about her own daughter, who was a doctor, an oncologist, and
who was married to another doctor, a surgeon. "Medical school education worth money. Film school? No," Mimi said.

A year ago, Lydia had learned that Mimi's grandson, Franklin, who
had entered Carnegie Mellon as an engineering major, had switched
his major to poetry, and this gave Lydia some ammunition. Whenever
Mimi started in on Lydia's family, Lydia began to talk about poetry and
Mimi would shut up. After all, how could someone like Mimi, whose
English was terrible, have a grandson who was a poet? Mimi had lived
in America for thirty years but spoke English like a newcomer. Lydia
hardly had an accent when she spoke English. When she'd arrived in
America forty years before, she had worked very hard to learn the language. She took evening ESL classes at the YWCA and she practiced
along with the television at home, repeating after the actors, even
during commercials.

The spotlight clicked off after Anna finished speaking and the
movie began. Anna's movie was about a Chinese woman who had married an American man and then the woman's short, ugly mother, who
was as pale and dumpy as a mushroom, moved in with the newlyweds.
In one scene the mother followed her daughter around the supermarket, took out groceries the daughter had placed in the cart, and substi-
tuted healthier items. Another scene showed the mother revacuuming
a carpet the daughter had just vacuumed. These were things that had
happened between Lydia and Anna, and Lydia could not believe Anna
would put their private business on display. Throughout the movie the
audience snorted with laughter as the mother meddled in the lives of
her daughter and the husband, and Lydia's chest felt heavy and tight.
This was what her daughter had spent the last three years writing and
directing and editing?

Yes, she'd been living with her daughter and son-in-law and grandchildren for ten years, but did her daughter really resent her so much and see her as such a busybody meddler that she had to make a movie about it? Eleven years ago Lydia's husband had left her broke when he died suddenly of a heart attack, their fabric shop in New York's Chinatown foundering because so few people still sewed their own clothing. She'd sold off the business and sold back the bolts of rich red and blue and green silk to wholesalers for a fraction of what she'd paid for them, and what she made was barely enough to climb out of bankruptcy. She had nowhere to go but to live with her only child in Pittsburgh, but she hated to leave New York, where she had friends and was important in her church and knew where to buy the freshest vegetables. Back then, she thought it might be all right to live with Anna and Gray. Her grandchildren were still babies, and she thought she could help raise them, especially since Anna did not see fit to stop working even though she'd had children. But what if during all these years Anna had resented Lydia, and this movie was her way of making this known to the world?

When the lights came back on, the crowd clapped loudly. Lydia felt hot and sweaty and wasn't sure she would be able to stand up without her knees buckling.

"Well, well," Mimi said. "Best movie I see in long, long, long time. I go tell Anna I hope movie get into every theater in whole country!"

Mimi jogged up to Anna, who was already surrounded by a swelling crowd. Mimi had left her purse under her chair, so Lydia reached down, opened Mimi's purse, took out the bag containing the ceramic Jesus, and slipped Jesus into her own purse. She stood up carefully, and once she was sure she had her balance, she marched over to Gray. She told him she had a pounding headache and could not stay in the hot gallery for one minute longer. She needed to be driven home immediately.

In the morning, Lydia watched as Anna poured coffee into a mug that looked like a soup bowl with a handle and then emptied four packets of Sweet'N Low into it. Anna had dark circles under her eyes from staying out too late the night before. So far Anna had not asked Lydia what she thought about the movie. Maybe she knew not to say anything. It was obvious now why Anna had tried so hard to get her to leave last night before the movie had even begun.

It was eight thirty, and Lydia needed to be dropped off at the church in an hour for a bazaar that Mimi had organized to raise money for victims of a hurricane down South. Lydia felt she had to participate in the bazaar because she knew that if she did not, Mimi would tell everyone that Lydia just did not care about anyone besides herself. Lydia had spent the last few weeks making scarves to sell, and she hoped she brought in far more money than Mimi would with whatever it was that she was planning on hawking. She wondered if Mimi would mention her missing Jesus while they were at the bazaar; if she did, Lydia would try to convince Mimi that she'd misplaced it and just couldn't remember where it was. One day she might sneak the Jesus back into Mimi's purse, but for now she felt like keeping it.

Hope and Chance rattled into the kitchen, still in their pajamas. Chance's hair stood up in all directions, and Hope was wearing a very unladylike Pirates baseball cap over her tangled hair. Lydia sipped jasmine tea and slowly ate a bowl of unsweetened oatmeal while she watched Anna drink another cup of coffee. She wanted to tell Anna that someone who was only five feet tall should not consume a gallon of coffee every day, but she was still not speaking to her daughter. She was unsure whether Anna had even noticed she was getting the silent treatment.

Hope reached for a box of Cap'n Crunch on a high shelf. She was tall and thin, taller even than Anna, and it was always her job to grab objects from high places. She poured some cereal into a bowl and threw the open box to Chance. He moved too slowly to catch it, and yellow balls of cereal rolled across the kitchen floor.

Lydia would never have fed Anna such an unhealthy breakfast when she was a child. Anna had eaten unsweetened oatmeal with raisins and a glass of orange juice for breakfast for the first seventeen years of her life. Every morning breakfast had been at seven thirty. And what had all that healthiness and structure led to? Nothing at all; Anna let her children eat whatever they wanted whenever they wanted, and now there were balls of sugary cereal rolling all over the kitchen floor.

"You two want to go to the church bazaar with your grandma and me?" Anna asked the kids. Since Lydia did not drive, Anna was supposed to drop her off.

"What's a bazaar?" Hope said.

"We're selling things on the church lawn," Lydia said. "To raise money."

"Is Mrs. Liu gonna be there?" Chance said, picking up a few pieces of cereal and throwing them into the trash. "I hate how she's always making fun of our names." Chance stood up as tall as he could, which wasn't very tall because he was short and plump, shaped like a sack of rice. He put his hands on his hips and imitated Mimi's harsh voice: "Hope and Chance? Not real names! Not real! No good!"

Hope and Anna laughed hard, and Lydia wanted to laugh because Chance sounded just like Mimi, but she smashed her lips tightly together to prevent herself from saying anything. It was rude to make fun of elders, no matter how obnoxious and noisy and dumb the elders were, and she did not want to set a bad example. She'd explained the names to Mimi—the twins had been born two and a half months premature, and once the family had learned they would be healthy and survive, Gray had chosen names he thought were meaningful.

"Well," Mimi had said, "what you expect from man named Gray? Gray is color, not name."

"So are you two coming to the bazaar?" Lydia said. "If not, I can walk there because you can't stay home alone."

"Don't be absurd, Ma. You're not walking three miles to the church," Anna said. "We're all going, OK?"

Lydia was silent for a few moments, then she nodded. She wanted to see how long it would be before her daughter realized she was not being spoken to.

At the bazaar, Lydia poured out her collection of scarves from a tote bag and stretched them across a folding table. Anna took the children on a walk around the church lawn and bought them lemonade and kettle corn, even though it was still morning. By noon, Lydia thought, the children would have consumed more sugar than she had eaten all year.

After Lydia set up her scarves, Mimi scuttled over to the table next to Lydia's, which was piled high with junky objects—old sweaters, rusty gardening tools, battered VHS tapes.

"This is your table?" Lydia said, eyeing the piles as if they contained dead birds that had been chewed up and spit out by a cat.

"Why you always follow me?" Mimi said.

Lydia turned away and rearranged her scarves. Anna brought the children to Lydia's table and waved at Mimi. Chance and Hope loudly chomped on kettle corn, and Mimi looked at them with disdain.

"Hi, Mrs. Liu. You did a great job organizing this bazaar," Anna said. Lydia was glad Anna was being polite, that she'd said Mrs. Liu instead of calling Mimi by her first name, but Mimi was probably thinking it was bad that Anna was not speaking Chinese. But Anna *could* speak it. Lydia had taught her daughter Chinese, even though she'd been born in America. But Anna never spoke it anymore, especially because she had no Chinese friends. The twins understood it, although they no longer spoke it either. When they were babies, Lydia had insisted on teaching them Mandarin—she'd heard that babies' brains absorbed languages in ways an adult brain never could—but once they'd started school, all they ever wanted to speak was English. Lydia had tried for a while to speak to them in Chinese, but they'd always respond in English. Eventually she gave up, tired of conversations that bounced back and forth between languages. Although she loved her grandchildren, sometimes they seemed so strange to her; even though they were half Chinese, they seemed not Chinese at all, raised on American food and TV, playing only with their American friends, not knowing anything about where they'd come from.

"How's Franklin?" Anna asked.

"Oh, Franklin, he so smart. He best in class."

"Best in his poetry class?" Lydia said. She could not help herself.

Mimi narrowed her eyes, speechless for just a moment. Then she spun toward Anna. "I tell everyone you make good movie about hating your mother."

"What?" Anna said.

"Nothing, nothing," Lydia said. "You know she doesn't understand English very well. She couldn't understand what was going on in your movie." How dare Mimi embarrass Lydia in front of her family? It was one thing for Mimi to whisper rude comments just to Lydia, but it was another thing entirely for her to try to shame her in front of her daughter.

"No, I understand Anna thinks you are pain in butt," said Mimi, grinning and pointing at her own rear.

"No, no," Anna said, waving her hands as if she were trying to erase a blackboard. "The *character* in the movie got a little annoyed at her mother, but the character isn't really me."

It was an easy way for Anna to explain things, but Lydia knew the truth: the mother in the movie *was* Lydia, and a joke had been made of her. Why had Anna wanted to hurt her? Surely Anna had to know that Lydia had only wanted the best for her, always. Yes, she'd been strict when Anna was growing up, but all she wanted was for Anna to grow up to be a proper, well-behaved young lady. All that time and effort, all those years of telling Anna to say please and thank you and to wipe her shoes on a mat before entering anyone's home and to always bring a small gift when invited to dinner. What had all that amounted to? That movie with the awful mother.

"Can we be models for you?" said Chance, as he picked up a scarf with his sticky fingers.

"OK," Lydia said, and Hope and Chance each wound a scarf around their necks. Chance's scarf was green and blue striped, and Hope's was pink and purple. Lydia wanted to tell Hope and Chance not to get the scarves sticky, but she was scared she'd sound like the mother in Anna's movie, so she said nothing.

Mimi smiled at Lydia and said, "I *hope* there is *chance* your scarves sell."

"Stupid old lady," whispered Chance, and Anna shushed him and told him and Hope to look at the other tables and see if there was anything they wanted to buy. She gave them each five dollars.

Instead of shopping, Hope and Chance marched up and down the church lawn, pestered people, spun their scarves around their necks, then unwound them, waving them around in the air like kites. They kept pointing to Lydia's table. It was good that the proceeds of the bazaar were for charity. Otherwise it would have been intolerable to see her grandchildren begging for customers, especially in Mimi's presence. Every once in a while Lydia shifted her gaze to Mimi's face and saw that she was looking at Hope and Chance with pursed lips. Anna moved to the next table and picked up an old book with yellowing pages and began to read.

After half an hour, Hope and Chance grew bored and returned to Lydia's table, so Anna took them to a café down the street where they could drink hot chocolate and do homework. Again, Lydia had to control herself; she wanted to tell Anna that the children had already had enough sugar, but she bit her lip and watched them walk away.

The day passed slowly, people poking around on the tables and mostly leaving empty-handed. By the end of the day, Mimi hadn't mentioned her missing Jesus; in fact, after Anna left, Mimi hadn't said anything more to Lydia. Lydia decided she would keep Jesus for a while, wait until Mimi started to talk about it, and then she'd find some way to slip it back into Mimi's purse. When Mimi found it, Lydia would say it had been there all along and Mimi was too dumb to notice a figurine squished in her purse among her tissues and cough drops and photographs of her poet grandson.

At dinner Lydia put the Jesus figurine on the table. "Look what I got at the bazaar today." It was a lie, but she couldn't very well tell her family she was a thief. When she got home from the bazaar, she'd gone to her room and seen Jesus on her dresser, staring up at her, open-palmed, judging her with his tiny brown eyes. She needed to get him out of her room.

"Is that a salt shaker?" Gray said, examining the top of Jesus's head.

"No!" snapped Lydia, taking Jesus out of Gray's hands.

"I just thought since he was on the table . . ."

"I think he might be valuable," Lydia said.

"*Antiques Roadshow* is going to be at the Convention Center next Saturday. I saw something on TV about it," Chance said. "You should take it there."

Lydia loved *Antiques Roadshow*. She liked seeing the surprise on people's faces when something they'd bought for a few dollars turned out to be worth thousands. She liked seeing all the strange things people found in their attics or garages. But mostly she liked the show because it was one of the programs she and her grandchildren could watch together and all be entertained.

Gray stared at the Jesus. "I don't know," he said. "It looks kind of ordinary. Like something you could buy anywhere."

Lydia suddenly wanted desperately to go see the appraisers at *Antiques Roadshow*, but she refused to beg to be taken there. Maybe she could figure out a bus route, sneak out of the house, and not tell anyone where she was going.

"Let me see," Anna said, taking the figurine from Lydia and examining it. "It seems well made. We should go get it appraised."

Lydia looked up from her broccoli, surprised. "Really?" she said, before realizing she'd broken her vow not to speak to her daughter.

"Why not?" Anna said. "It could be fun."

Lydia was unsure whether Anna really thought the Jesus might be valuable or whether she was trying to be extra nice after the things Mimi had said at the bazaar.

"Cool," Hope said. "Maybe we can get on TV."

"Maybe you'll want to brush your hair then," Lydia said. "Both of you. You don't want to get on TV and then have the world think you don't own a comb, do you?"

She caught Hope and Chance rolling their eyes at each other and she thought that later, when they were out of earshot, they'd make fun of her, the same way they'd made fun of Mimi that morning.

That night Lydia lay in bed and thought about the Jesus. Gray was probably right; it did look like something that could be purchased anywhere, and most likely it wasn't worth much. But what if it was valuable? Lydia knew exactly what she would do if she had thousands of dollars: she'd take her family to China. None of them had been there, and she could be their guide, could be important. In China, if Lydia stopped talking to Anna for a day, Anna would realize she was being ignored. And who knew—maybe after the trip Anna might even want to make a documentary about discovering her roots and learning to understand her mother. Lydia would show Anna the graves of her parents—Anna's grandparents, whom she'd never met—and they would all pay their respects, and Lydia would clean the stones and decorate the area with flowers to show that even though she now lived far away, she still thought of them often.

Lydia knew China wasn't the same as when she'd left. She had seen a documentary on television about Chinese teenagers with their love of McDonald's and video games and violent American movies, but there would be something important about showing her family where she'd come from. She would take them to the yam farm where her husband had grown up, tell them how he and his brothers would chase after the turkeys that ran through the property and if they caught and killed one, their mother would pluck it and cook it and they'd eat turkey meat for a week. Chance and Hope would probably screw up their faces and say, "Gross," but Lydia would ask them what they thought their Thanksgiving turkeys looked like before the skin was crispy and browned and sliced with an electric knife.

After the yam farm, Lydia would show them the house she had grown up in, although it was no longer a house. A third cousin had written her a few years back and told her it had been torn down and a Pizza Hut had been constructed where the house once was. But it was still the same land, and she'd tell them that it was there, in the house that no longer stood, that she'd learned to read, taught by mission-aries. She would tell Gray that the missionaries really weren't doing something so different from what he did in the Peace Corps in Af-rica after college. She'd tell him she didn't care that he and Anna were atheists. Couldn't he see that without the missionaries she might be a very different person? She might have worked hard on her family's farm and died young, like her mother, and she might not have set out to America in search of better opportunities. She'd tell Anna about her favorite missionary couple, Thomas and Annabelle Fulton, who were from Wisconsin, both of them blond and patient and gentle-voiced, and tell her how Annabelle had read her stories from an illustrated children's Bible, read them over and over until Lydia recognized each word on her own. And she'd tell Anna something she'd never told her before: she'd tell her that she was named after Annabelle. And maybe Anna would scream at her, tell her she had some nerve naming her after a Christian missionary. And then maybe Anna's next movie wouldn't be a documentary about discovering her roots, but instead would be a drama featuring a harsh older lady, a religious zealot, and the most intense scene would be a confrontation between the woman and her atheist daughter about the daughter being named after a mis-sionary. After a screaming match, the daughter would march herself down to the Social Security office and change her name to something awful, like Rainbow or Stream. But it wouldn't matter, none of it, if Lydia could bring her family to China and show them something of the past.

The next Saturday, Gray drove the family to the Convention Cen-ter. Anna wore her usual weekend outfit—gray sneakers, baggy cam-ouflage pants, and a black sweater—but Hope and Chance had put on the clothes they'd worn on picture day at school. Chance's black dress pants were slightly too small for him. Hope wore a red dress with a bow in the back. Lydia noted with satisfaction that both had neatly combed their hair. Lydia wore a proper brown suit with a crisply ironed white shirt underneath. She'd finished off the outfit with her jade necklace.

Secretly, she hoped one of the appraisers would notice the necklace and comment on its quality, and she would get to share the story of how her grandmother had passed it down to her the night before she got married.

The Convention Center's parking lot was jammed with cars, and people marched toward the entrance in messy clumps, all clutching their prized possessions with looks of hopeful determination. Gray drove toward the entrance to drop the family off. He had to teach his intermediate glassblowing class but would be back in a few hours to pick them up. "Maybe we'll be millionaires by the time I return," he said, laughing, but Lydia did not laugh. She stared out the window and wondered what if, after all this, the Jesus was worthless? And then she squinted to make sure she was seeing correctly. Mimi Liu's ugly gold Mercedes with the Carnegie Mellon sticker placed crookedly in the rear window pulled into the parking lot. Franklin was at the wheel and Mimi was in the passenger seat. Lydia's heart beat faster: what would Mimi say if she saw that Lydia had the Jesus? Perhaps the space inside would be large and crowded enough that they could avoid bumping into each other.

It was swarming indoors, a whir of conversations about where objects had been found and the prices. Some people slogged toward the exits, dejected and sad-eyed. The fluorescent lights illuminated soundmen hefting enormous microphones over their heads. Lydia searched for Mimi and Franklin but could not find them.

Lydia, Anna, Hope, and Chance were directed to a snaking line of people. When they got to the front of the line, Lydia would talk to someone who would determine where her object came from and send her off to the proper appraiser.

"I bet we get on TV," said Hope, looking around the room. "I don't see anyone else with a Jesus."

Chance looked at the cameramen who rushed around the room. He patted down his cowlick and straightened his shirt.

"I know that guy!" Anna said, pointing to a gangly cameraman wearing faded jeans and a plaid shirt who was across the room filming a man who was having a book appraised. "We went to film school together. I'll be right back."

Lydia watched Anna walk across the room. When the man finished filming his segment, Anna tapped him on the shoulder. He handed his camera to another man, and he and Anna embraced. This, thought Lydia, was highly inappropriate behavior for a married woman in public. What if another cameraman caught this on film? What if it was shown on television? Worse, what if Mimi walked by and saw?

"Please have your items out and easily visible," yelled a woman carrying a clipboard. Lydia carefully extracted the Jesus from her purse and gripped it in her left hand.

"I bet Jesus will be worth something," said Chance. "Like five, no, six thousand dollars. If he's that valuable, will you buy me a dirt bike?"

"We'll see," Lydia said.

"How much did you say you paid for him?" Hope asked.

Before Lydia could come up with an answer, she felt a hard shove on her arm. "You thief!"

Lydia turned. There stood Mimi in another bright flowered dress. Franklin, whose spiky hair was pushed back by a pair of sunglasses atop his head, stood next to Mimi. He held a blue vase, which was decorated with intricate depictions of gold dragons, their long bodies swirled around the vase. He glared at his grandmother, who squawked like an angry crow.

"You steal Jesus!" Mimi shouted. Several people in line turned to look.

"This?" Lydia said innocently, looking down at the figurine in her hand. She'd been caught. And worst of all, it had happened in front of her family. What little respect they had for her had surely just evaporated. She had to try to save herself. "This is my Jesus."

"You stole it?" said Chance.

"That is so cool," said Hope.

Mimi grabbed the figurine out of Lydia's hand and waved it in the air.

"Stupid thief!" She flung the figure at Lydia, but Lydia did not raise her hands, and the Jesus bounced off her stomach and shattered on the floor. It seemed as if everyone in the Convention Center stopped talking. A camera crew rushed to the scene.

"Not valuable!" Mimi shouted, waving away the cameras. "Junk!"

Lydia watched Jesus's head spin around and around until it finally came to a stop in front of her black shoes.

"What's going on?" said Anna, who was breathing hard from rushing across the large room.

"Oh, you done with new boyfriend?" said Mimi.

"He's not—never mind," said Anna. "What's all this screaming about?"

Mimi pointed to Lydia and said, "She stole my Jesus. And so stupid because Jesus only worth two dollar! Stupid, stupid!"

"God, Grandmother," Franklin said, "you are totally making a scene. Could you turn down the volume?" He flipped his sunglasses onto his face, then twisted his head to look at the people around him. "I might know someone here."

"Ma, why'd you take that?" Anna whispered.

"I was going to return it." This was worse than Mimi mocking Anna's movie. Now Lydia was the bad one, which seemed impossible. Since she'd stolen the Jesus, she had been lying, and she was not a liar. She always did the right thing, she was always polite and had impeccable manners and she had never stolen a single thing in her life. When Anna was six and had taken a pack of gum from Woolworth's without paying, Lydia had made Anna return the gum and apologize. She'd been upset when the boy at the counter had said, "No biggie, kid. People steal this stuff all the time." That wasn't the point—people might steal things, but not people in the Wong family.

"Thief!" Mimi spat out again.

"Let's just go," said Lydia, pushing Chance and Hope by the shoulders. If she couldn't magically disappear, she could at least get out of this room, go home, shut her door, and figure out how she would go forth with life after this humiliation.

"Wait," Anna said, holding up a hand. "Stop. Everyone stop."

Lydia paused, her hands still on her grandchildren's shoulders. People were staring. It was a spectacle, and Lydia hated being part of it.

"Liu tài tai," Anna said, and Lydia was shocked to hear Anna say "Mrs. Liu" in Chinese. It was just the right thing to do, though; nobody around them could understand, and their business would remain their own. Anna continued speaking in Mandarin: "With all due respect, I don't understand why you give my mother such a hard time. I know you don't respect my work or my husband's work, but that's no reason to make fun of my mother. She's done nothing to you, except take that Jesus, and I would be happy to repay you for it."

Lydia smiled. Anna's Chinese had been perfect, the tones precise, amazing for someone born in this country. And she'd been polite and respectful.

"What'd she say?" Franklin said to Mimi.

Mimi shot Franklin an enraged look. Although Mimi had never admitted it, it was now clear that Franklin did not understand a word of Chinese.

Anna reached into one of the big pockets of her camouflage pants and took out her wallet. She counted out two one-dollar bills and put the money in Mimi's hand.

"What in the world is going on?" Franklin said. "What's the money for?"

Lydia felt something for Mimi then—pity, perhaps? No, something different. Sympathy? Maybe. She knew Mimi was ashamed that it had been publicly revealed that Franklin could not speak Chinese.

"This vase is totally getting heavy," Franklin said, clumsily setting it on the floor next to the Jesus's head. The vase wobbled for a moment, and Lydia was worried it might topple over.

Lydia looked at the vase from hundreds of years ago on the dirty floor and brought her hand to her jade necklace. She could appreciate Mimi's vase and Mimi could, surely, see what a lovely necklace Lydia owned, but could their families see the value in these things they'd treasured for so long? Shouldn't Franklin have known not to put something so old and important on the floor? One day, if Lydia gave her necklace to Hope, would she just hide it away in a dark drawer?

"I'll call Gray and see if he can pick us up now," said Anna. She reached down and took Chance and Hope's hands. "We can wait for him outside."

"Mom," Chance said, wiggling his arm. "We're too old to hold your hands."

"Please," said Anna, and Lydia saw how tired she looked. "Let's just go."

"You go call Gray," Lydia said. "I'll meet you outside in a few minutes."

"Are you sure?" Anna said, looking from Lydia to Mimi. "You want to stay here?"

"I can stay with you," Hope said.

"You all go. I'll be out soon," Lydia said. She felt grateful for her family's concern, but there was more that needed to be said to Mimi. Anna, Chance, and Hope left the crowded room, and Lydia looked at Mimi, who stared down into the neck of the vase. Then Mimi turned and marched toward the exit. Lydia reached down and picked up the vase.

"Hey, that doesn't belong to you," said Franklin, but Lydia ignored him.

She hurried to catch up to Mimi. She followed Mimi down a hallway and then around a corner. She followed her up an escalator and down another hallway. Finally, Mimi heaved herself into a black leather chair. Lydia placed the vase gently in Mimi's lap, and then she sat in another chair a few feet away.

"Still always follow me, huh?" said Mimi, wrapping her arms around the vase.

Lydia did not say anything for a few moments. How could she talk about anything that had just happened? How could speaking make the situation better? They'd both been shamed, but how could either of them talk about the things that humiliated them? Finally, she said, "I heard the market is getting scallops this week."

Mimi did not speak immediately, as if she were weighing her answer carefully. "Bay or sea?" Mimi asked.

"Sea," said Lydia.

"Good," said Mimi. "Bay too small. They cook too fast and taste like eraser."

Lydia wanted to say that, in fact, bay scallops were sweeter than sea scallops, but they had to be attended to more carefully. She could imagine Mimi emptying a sack of scallops into a hot pan, turning around to yell at Franklin for a few minutes, and returning to the pan to find the scallops charred and rubbery. But this was not the time to tell Mimi she should pay attention when cooking scallops.

"Frozen or fresh?" Mimi asked.

"Frozen, I think," said Lydia.

"Frozen seafood no good," said Mimi, shaking her head. "You can always tell when you eat if seafood been frozen before." She paused for a moment, sighed, then said, "But that's life. Can't always get what you want."

Lydia nodded.

Mimi stood with the vase cradled in her arms. "I got to go. Things to do."

Lydia stood up too.

"Maybe I see you Tuesday at market," Mimi said. "Maybe we both get scallops, even if not too good."

"I'll be there," said Lydia.

Lydia watched Mimi shuffle down the hall and disappear around a corner. After a few moments, she headed down the hall too. On the escalator from the first floor to the lobby, Lydia could see the glass doors leading to the sidewalk outside. When she got to the bottom of the escalator, she saw Anna, Hope, and Chance waiting on the sidewalk, their backs to the building. Chance leaned against Anna, even though a few minutes before he'd told her he didn't want to hold her hand. Anna reached her left arm up and draped it around Hope's shoulder. The automatic doors slid open, and Lydia stepped into the warmth of the afternoon to join her family.

Designated Driver

You're a bus driver now. And tonight is Halloween, which means drunk college students riding the bus to and from parties. Eventually someone will make a mess—vomit, vampire makeup smeared on a window, a can of soda sloshed on the floor—and it's your job to clean it up, even though you've written numerous lengthy letters to the Transit Authority regarding the fact that you're a bus driver, not a maid, and someone should be hired to clean the buses.

On Fourth Street, Frankenstein steps up with his too-large black platform shoes and trips on the third step. He flails for the handrail and reaches it just in time. A smudge of green body paint remains on the silver handrail after he climbs the steps.

At the next stop, two nurses enter the bus, and you hope the second one, the one with flat-ironed hair and scrubs with pink bunnies on them, doesn't recognize you. She was there the second and third time you went to the emergency room to get your stomach pumped; she was the one who'd gently inserted the tube down your throat, administered the saline solution, and told you it was going to be OK as you waited for the fluid to clear. You remember that her name is Connie. She flashes her bus pass and walks by quickly and doesn't look at you.

The nurses are dressed in scrubs, but they have only small purses with them, and their hair and makeup is done, so they are not going to the hospital for a night shift but to a Halloween party, dressed as nurses. Although this nurse has seen your humiliation, twice, her lack of imagination regarding her costume somehow makes you feel better about things.

On Eighth Street, four college-aged guys step onto the bus through the back door. Passengers are supposed to enter through the front door and exit through the back. The boys are wearing straw hats, overalls buckled over bare torsos, and bandanas tied around their necks. The last boy that gets on the bus has curly red hair poking out from under his hat and is carrying a baby potbellied pig. He's arrogant about it, doesn't even try to hide the pig, and you immediately dislike him.

"You can't get on the bus through the back door," you tell them, watching their reflections in the rearview mirror. You don't want to turn around because you don't want the nurse to see your face, so you say it facing forward.

"What?" shouts one of the boys, whose head is shaped like a potato. You tilt the rearview mirror. Connie is talking to her friend. This is a college town. You're sure she's seen her share of alcohol poisonings. It's been over a year since you last saw her. She's probably seen thousands of patients since then; the chances are slim that she'd remember your face. You turn around.

"We're already on the bus. Do you want us to get off and then get back on through the front door?" says the smallest of the boys, the only one without muscular arms. Why is he with the others? In another situation, you might guess he's the designated driver, but tonight you're everyone's designated driver. His question seems earnest, and you wonder whether he's a nice boy or just simpleminded.

"Come up here and show me your passes," you say. They walk up and each flash their college ID, which gets them free bus rides. "You can't have an animal on the bus," you say. They're not allowed, and besides, you don't like animals anymore.

"It's a seeing eye pig," says the redhead.

"It's part of our costume," says the little one.

"Are you guys supposed to be strippers?" you say, although you know they are not.

"Uh, *farmers*," the potato-headed one says, pointing to the red bandana tied around his neck, as if this is some sort of well-known symbol for farmers.

"What are you supposed to be?" the redhead says. "Like, a bus driver?" One of the boys, whose pointy-nosed face reminds you of a ferret, laughs a hard, wheezy laugh. His head is too small for his over-muscled body.

"Miss?" says a thin older woman wearing a laminated ID card hanging around her neck by a string. "Could we please go? I'm going to be late." She's probably a night shift worker, maybe a janitor on her way to clean a building at night. She, like you, is one of the invisibles, one of the people who keep things running. You don't want her to be late.

You pull the lever that shuts the doors, and the shirtless farmers and their pig walk to the back of the bus. Two of the boys have tattoos on their upper arms: Potato Head has Chinese characters, and Ferret Face has some sort of tribal band circling his bicep. The tattoos don't make them look exotic or interesting; they make them look even more like suburban white boys.

The four boys take up the entire back row of the bus, and the red-head puts the pig down. It's not on a leash. When you pull up to the next stop, you turn around and see it totter and fall and struggle to right itself. It keeps sliding toward the front of the bus. Passengers in costumes are reaching out to touch it, and it's squealing and unhappy.

"Get your pig under control," you say, and the boy with the thin arms leans down, grabs the pig's front legs, and drags it to the rear of the bus. The pig squeals the whole way.

"Shut up, piggy!" shouts Potato Head, and you wonder if these boys have been too lazy to even name the pig. The skinny-armed boy picks up the pig and settles it in his lap. He pets it like it's a cat, and the other boys laugh at him.

For a while things are quiet, and you round the corner toward downtown, and the passengers empty out of the bus. First the nurses leave and then Frankenstein and then a pack of girls who smell like cigarettes and are all wearing tight black dresses and cat ears. Finally the woman with the laminated ID around her neck disappears into an office building. Soon it's just you and the four boys and the pig, and you drive toward the west end of the university.

Ferret Face pulls a small bag of chocolate chip cookies out of his pocket, shoves a few into his mouth, and tosses one down the aisle. The pig scrambles for the cookie and falls once again. The boys laugh hard. They throw more cookies, and the pig chases after them, falling and grunting and rolling onto its back. This is not normal behavior for a pig. You suspect this pig is drunk, fed cheap alcohol. You know pigs will eat just about anything, but they shouldn't ever be given cookies. There is special food that is made for pigs. It comes in pellets that look like dog food. Pigs can also eat vegetables. They should not eat too much starch.

You know these things because two years ago you were in veterinary school. You were good at what you did; you were going to be a surgeon for small animals. You'd always had steady hands, and when you were young your mother said you'd either be a surgeon or a painter. You were never good at art and always liked animals more than people, so veterinary school made sense. But then the stress of school got to you, and drinking was the only thing that could relax you. There were the three trips to the emergency room to get your stomach pumped, and then the man you lived with called you incredibly irresponsible and broke up with you and moved out, and then you began to drink even more heavily.

On weekends you volunteered at the shelter; you neutered and spayed cats for free. You were flunking out of school, but you were helping animals, so you told yourself you weren't a total failure. You knew you should have stopped when your hands started shaking, but you'd performed these surgeries so many times that you could do it with shaky hands.

Then there was the white cat. Her abdomen had been shaved and she was ready for you. Your head pounded and you couldn't focus your eyes. You made the incision through the skin and abdominal muscles, and the line your scalpel made was crooked, but you kept going. You'd meant to remove just the ovaries and uterus, but you slipped and the scalpel plunged into her stomach. There was no reasonable way to save her. Since she was already anesthetized, you opened her chest cavity, injected the sodium pentobarbital intercardially. The next day, you dropped out of school. In the two years since, you haven't trusted yourself to touch an animal, not even a quick pat when a dog runs up to you in the park. You've spent the last two years thinking you're dangerous, poison to animals.

And now? You have stopped drinking because you are not stupid. You can mess up your own life, but you cannot risk the lives of an entire bus full of passengers. There's one thing you can be proud of: you've never driven drunk. You have no tolerance for people who hurt others.

"Get off the bus," you say. "And leave the pig. You can't have it."

"My dad's a lawyer," says the redhead. "He'll sue you. Do you know how much we paid for this pig? You can't just take it."

"My dad's an animal rights attorney. He'll get *you* for what you did to the pig," you say. This is not true—your father owns a sporting goods store—but your lie makes the redhead's skin blanch paler than it already is. This is what you don't tell him: the pig will be OK. Animals that live outdoors sometimes get drunk. They eat fruit that has fallen off trees and fermented on the ground. Many deer have gotten drunk on cherries and apples and then wobbled around for a few hours. But they survive.

"Get off the bus," you say again, forcing your voice to be as firm as you can make it, and to your surprise all four boys storm off. Only the littlest one turns to look back. The rest stomp toward a dorm that is decorated on the outside with clusters of orange and black balloons.

Once they are gone, the pig sidles up to you, leans hard into your leg, and you feel its warm body through the fabric of your pants. You turn the bus around, but you're not going to finish your route. You will take care of the pig tonight, make sure it's OK, give it water, make sure it safely sleeps off the alcohol. You'll make it a bed with old towels folded into a large cardboard box. In the morning, you will go buy it food. This is your pig now.

The Local Scrooge

Usually the weeks between the end of Thanksgiving break and the start of winter break were a time of restless quiet on the campus of Willard College. Students were eager to finish the first semester and head home for a month off, and professors were busy grading final assignments and exams. But this year was different. A burst of energy had been infused into Willard's campus because of a simple mistake that greatly mortified Pete Peterson, professor of English. And it wasn't even his mistake! This was the fault of Paul Peterson (no relation) in the Philosophy Department and Pete's own daughter, Wendy, in Chicago. Paul had acted with malice, but Wendy—most likely—had not.

Pete sat in his office and angrily chomped on pretzel sticks he yanked out of a foot-tall plastic barrel. He tore through the pretzels, feeling only momentary bolts of satisfaction when salt hit his tongue. He knew that when he ate in anger he got crumbs in his mustache, but he didn't care. He ate and ate, sending crumbs and crystals of salt everywhere, and he did not stop until all the pretzels had been consumed. He shook the salt on the bottom of the container into the trash can under his desk and then marched, empty pretzel barrel in hand, into the office of the department's administrative coordinator, Ida.

Ida smiled at him, failing to conceal a knowing grin. So she'd seen the horrible mistake too. "You're a sweetheart, Pete. Don't try to hide it," she said. Pete huffed and swept a Sharpie out of the clay mug on her desk, where she kept her writing utensils. When he'd once asked why she had such a crooked, ugly thing on her desk, she'd told him her granddaughter had made it for her in a pottery class and she thought it was beautiful.

On the pretzel barrel, Pete wrote TIPS in large black letters, then he slammed the Sharpie back into Ida's mug.

"Bless your heart, Pete Peterson!" Ida shouted as Pete scurried to his noon composition class.

Once in the classroom, he looked at the students, keeping his eyes focused over all their heads, not meeting any of their gazes. He knew they were staring at him, eyes wide, and that they'd been talking about him before he entered the classroom. "I want to know," he declared, focusing on a dent in the back wall, "whether you think you've learned from me this semester. Have I rendered a service to you, and have I rendered it well? You don't need to tell me in words, but I'm leaving this here, right on the desk, and you put in what you think is appropriate." He slammed his empty plastic barrel on the desk, and the thumping hollow sound it made reverberated through the room. "Now, I'm not asking for fifteen to twenty percent of the tuition you paid to attend this class—that would be ludicrous—but what am I worth to you? Take a minute and think and put in what you consider is my appropriate tip for this semester's teaching. I'm leaving now, and I'll be back at the end of the class period. You can go once you've left your tip." And with that, Pete stomped out of the classroom, proud that he'd managed to not look a single student in the eye during the entire performance.

A week earlier, Pete had been in Chicago visiting his daughter and her family. He'd flown out for Thanksgiving, after Wendy pestered him for months and months to come visit. "You need to meet Milo," she'd said. "You know, Mom flew out right after he was born. Don't you even *want* to meet him? Genetically, he's like twenty-five percent you."

Mom was Pete's ex-wife, Laurie, and Pete was sure Wendy knew that the most certain way to get him to do anything was to mention Laurie and try to create some competition between them.

Pete had worried that he would not like Milo. And it was wrong, wasn't it, for a man to not have feelings of warmth for his firstborn grandchild? He'd seen pictures, which Wendy sent in a thick envelope each month, and the boy looked just like Wendy's idiot husband, Gary. Same round head, same pink cheeks, same eyelashes that looked too long to possibly belong to a male of the human species. The two of them—Milo with his hair yet to grow in, and Gary with his balding head—looked like those dolls Wendy used to play with when she was a child, those Kewpie dolls with their bulging bellies and permanent looks of stoned bemusement.

"Fine, fine," Pete had said. "I'll book the flight, but you know I hate flying in general and I especially hate flying during the holidays when everyone is sniffling and sneezing and bringing their germs into the recirculated air."

"Excellent," Wendy said. "I'll send you some vitamin C."

"We have vitamin C in Indiana," Pete said. "You think we're all walking around with scurvy?"

Wendy always asked him when he was planning on retiring and getting out of Willard, and he felt he needed to defend his home, although it was not a place he particularly liked. Wendy had grown up there, had developed a passionate resentment for the provincial attitudes and insularity of the town, and had left for college and tried her best to stay away from Willard. She said life was more exciting in the city, easier in many ways. You didn't have to drive everywhere, there were lots of ethnic restaurants, the museums were fabulous, there was public transportation. "You think I *like* public transportation?" Pete always replied.

Although Willard wasn't ideal, it was certainly better than living in a city. He didn't want to wait on a dirty street corner with a bus schedule in his hand, didn't want to be shoehorned into some too-crowded El train, didn't want to be pushed so close to other commuters that he could smell stale breath and sweaty armpits. He liked the privacy and sanctity of his car, enjoyed driving his Prius with the Obama '12 bumper sticker among the dirty, backfiring pickup trucks in Willard. He didn't mind the rude shouts in the Walmart parking lot when people spat out comments like "*Your* president is ruining this country," and he especially liked driving past the house with the Confederate flag being used as a patch for a shattered window and honking his horn loudly and sticking up his middle finger as he passed. Pete was not a nice man—this was the one thing in the world he knew to be wholly true—but he also knew he had a keen sense of what was just and fair and right, and he wanted everyone to know where he stood politically and socially. In Chicago he'd be nothing special, just another liberal among many, but in Willard he felt unique and important, felt as if he was making some sort of ripple in the complacent heartland. Willard was home, and Willard College, where he'd been teaching English for over thirty years, was familiar and he relished his role as the faculty grump, the one person who could always be counted on to disagree at a meeting. There was no way, ever, that he'd move to Chicago and leave behind the town where he'd settled in as the local scrooge, the grinch, the mean old guy.

At O'Hare, Wendy waited for Pete at the luggage carousel, the baby slung in some sort of flowered sack across her chest. Pete wanted to ask Wendy if she'd mugged a hippie to get that contraption, but before he could say anything, she shouted, "It's Grandpa!" She jumped up and down, and Milo jiggled a bit, and Pete ran to them, afraid the baby would drop out of the sack, and he put his hands under the fat curve of Milo's back. He thought how much the hunk of baby felt like the hunk of pork shoulder he'd held up in the supermarket the other day, had cradled lovingly for a few moments before remembering the list of foods his doctor had told him a man his age should avoid.

"Dad," Wendy said, reaching around the baby to hug him. "What an unexpected show of affection."

Pete realized he was still clutching the baby, still thinking of the pork shoulder, and he released the baby and let his arms hang at his sides.

"Milo, this is your grandpa," Wendy said, and, using just one hand while the other held the baby, undid a complicated knot on the pouch. She removed the baby and pouch from her body and turned Milo to face Pete.

"Oh!" Pete said, stunned. The baby had his eyes; this was a fact. His own brown eyes peeking out from beneath those ridiculous eyelashes that looked like they belonged on a giraffe. "He looks a little like me."

"His eyes, right?" Wendy said, and Pete nodded. The baby reached for Pete's mustache and ran his fingers through it and giggled. And then he started laughing hard, deep belly laughs that seemed impossible coming out of someone so small. Pete was—what? What was he? The only word he could think of was "delighted," but Pete Peterson was most certainly not the type of man who was ever delighted, and he wished he could find a better word for the way he felt.

"Can you say hi to Grandpa?" Wendy asked.

Of course the child couldn't. He was six months old. He could barely hold his own head up and keep the spit inside his mouth.

"Why don't you take him and I'll get your suitcases," Wendy said. She handed Milo to Pete before he could refuse, and when Milo landed on his chest, Pete smelled the baby smell, the combination of powder and tear-free shampoo and some unnamable sweetness, and he remembered when Wendy was this small and how much he had loved having someone so little who depended on him so much. But he'd been a different man then, a softer man; this was before his marriage had turned sour, before thirty-two years of teaching had hardened him the way a callus hardened on a foot. It was a gross image, Pete knew, but he thought of himself this way, hardened from overuse. At sixty-two, Pete was not a man who wanted anything to do with babies.

But here was Milo, still laughing, still touching his mustache, and Pete thought perhaps it was good that Wendy had married Gary, who, although he annoyed Pete, had a pleasant disposition. Wendy had been a colicky child who'd turned into a difficult teenager and a sarcastic, moody adult. This baby seemed to have nothing of Wendy in him. Pete blew a small stream of air into the baby's face, and at first Milo looked surprised, his eyes wide. Why had Pete done this? This was what he did to his cat when she misbehaved: a quick, hard stream of air in the cat's face, and she'd jump off the counter or retract her claws and stop using the couch as a scratching post. Why had he done this to the baby who had done nothing wrong? But then Milo smiled, a wet, gummy grin, and another deep belly laugh emerged, and Pete Peterson could not help but laugh along with his grandson.

The next day, Wendy took Pete to her favorite ice cream boutique. What had happened to the word "parlor," Pete thought, or even the simple, utilitarian word "shop"? When they stepped inside, Pete said, "Well, now I know why they call it a boutique. Use a fancy word and you can charge six bucks for a scoop of ice cream."

"Dad, please," Wendy said, shifting Milo in his flowered carrying sack. "You're not in Willard anymore."

"You can say that again," Pete said, surveying the flavors, which had been printed in multicolored chalk on a giant chalkboard that hung behind the counter. Caramel with Himalayan pink sea salt? Lavender mint? For God's sake, goat cheese with Alpine strawberries and cardamom? There was a large sign on the wall announcing that the milk the ice cream was made from was organic, and most of the ingredients were sourced from local farms. "I just want strawberry," Pete said. "Regular old strawberry. Maybe even made with artificial flavor. And red dye #40."

"That's not possible," Wendy said. She scanned the giant chalkboard and said, "How about strawberry champagne rosemary?"

Finally, Pete settled on an ice cream that was made with beer, a porter. He licked his cone as Wendy deliberated over what she wanted. His ice cream was OK, had a hint of chocolate, but it was not worth six dollars. And he still would have preferred strawberry. Wendy ordered a basil lemon sorbet to share with Milo. When they got to the register, Pete reached for his wallet, but Wendy said, "I got it." Their two servings of ice cream cost thirteen dollars with tax. Wendy handed the girl at the counter a ten and a five and the girl gave Wendy back two singles. Wendy dropped the singles into a large glass jar next to the cash register. A notecard taped to the jar read, "Tipping is good karma!" The girl at the register had turned her back by the time Wendy's singles floated down the jar, and Pete thought, *If you put money in a tip jar and no one sees or hears you do it, does it count?* It was like the old "if a tree falls in the forest" conundrum but worse, because who really cared about trees falling in forests? Everyone cared about wasted money. Didn't they?

When they sat down on pink plastic chairs at the back of the shop, Pete whispered, "What was the tip for?"

Wendy lifted a spoonful of sorbet to Milo's mouth and said, "They're probably college students. They could use the cash more than I could."

"But what did you tip for? Scooping ice cream into a cup? They didn't even have to deliver our food to a table!"

Wendy shrugged. "They got our orders correct."

"They only had to remember them for two seconds! They get paid, you know."

Milo opened his mouth wide, ready for more sorbet. "You like it, don't you, pumpkin?" Wendy said. She cooed at Milo and fed him another small spoonful.

"What baby likes basil?" Pete said.

"*My* baby," Wendy said. "I'm training his palate to be more sophisticated than mine was. I'm not raising him on hot dogs and meatloaf."

"Well excuse me," Pete said. "Money doesn't grow on trees." And then he was mad at himself for letting such a blatant cliché pour out of his mouth. He was always circling clichés on his students' papers, circling them again and again in red ink, sometimes circling so hard and vigorously the paper ripped and his red ink slid onto the next page. And now he was thinking of money on trees and trees falling in forests. He'd only been away from school for three days and already his mind was turning to mush. No, no, not turning to mush. He needed a better, more original way of saying this.

"My brain is turning into a puddle of overpriced frou-frou ice cream," Pete said.

"What?" Wendy said.

"Never mind," Pete said, noticing his ice cream had begun to melt down his arm.

On Wednesday, Wendy took Pete and Milo to her favorite coffee shop. "Milo loves gumming their biscotti," she said. Again there was a menu written in pastel-colored chalk behind the register. Everything was flavored and frothy and infused with cinnamon or vanilla or hazelnut.

"You know what you want, sir?" said the boy behind the counter, who had a ring in his eyebrow and another in his lip.

"How do you talk with that in?" Pete asked.

Wendy sighed loudly.

"This one's not the problem," the boy said. He opened his mouth and stuck his tongue out. There was a metal rod with a ball on the end of it in the middle of his tongue. "This one took some getting used to."

An uncomfortable shiver slid down Pete's spine. "But why?" Pete said. "Why would you do something like this to yourself?"

The boy shrugged.

"You won't always be young, you know. One day you'll be my age. Then what will you do with all the extra holes in your body?"

The boy laughed. "You sound like my dad," he said.

"I bet you can't imagine being my age, but it happens faster than you know," Pete said. "Imagine me with a ring in my eyebrow. How silly would that look? People would laugh."

"All right, Dad," Wendy said. "Do you know what you want?"

"Just coffee. Just plain old coffee. Is that possible?" he said to the boy.

"Definitely," the boy said, placing an empty mug on the counter.

"I'll have one too," Wendy said, and the boy placed another empty mug next to the first one.

"Is this *invisible* coffee?" Pete said, looking into the mug.

"It's over there," Wendy said. She pointed to a bar across the room, with five silver carafes lined up on it.

"All you can drink," the boy said. "Try the new Indonesian. It's awesome."

"Do you still have the Kenyan?" Wendy said.

"Always," said the boy. He rang up their two coffees and the biscotti for Milo. Then, again, Wendy dropped two dollars into a tip jar. This time it wasn't a jar, though; it was a giant coffee mug. The boy didn't acknowledge Wendy's tip, although he surely saw her put the money in.

Pete picked up both mugs by the handles, and Wendy carried the plate with Milo's biscotti to a table in the corner. He filled Wendy's mug with the coffee from Kenya. The card on the carafe read, "Taste the smooth warmth of the Kenyan plains! Hints of cherry and smoke with a woodsy undertone." He studied the rest of the coffee selection: Vanillaberry, Butterscotch Crumpet, Blueberry Fields, Indonesian. He sighed and pushed the button on top of the Indonesian carafe as he read the attached card. "Enjoy the lush green vibrancy of the rainforest! A touch of banana and cinnamon with a taste of nutmeg." Coffee was getting worse than wine, Pete thought. Coffee was supposed to taste like coffee, bitter and strong and nothing more.

Pete brought the mugs back to their table and saw that Milo had drenched one end of the biscotti with drool. He realized he'd forgotten napkins.

"I didn't know if you wanted milk or sugar," Pete said.

"Skim, but I'll get it. You want any?" Wendy said. Pete shook his head. Wendy got up and poured milk into her mug and returned to the table. Once she was back watching Milo in his highchair, Pete got up and brought a stack of napkins back to the table.

"That's a lot of effort we had to expend to get this coffee, huh?"

"Please, Dad," Wendy said, then she took a sip of her coffee. "Is this about the tip again?"

"He didn't even pour anything! He gave us mugs."

"He was nice to you. He let you ask him about his piercings."

"That doesn't warrant a tip. Should I have tipped the lady who sat next to me on the plane? She let me ask her about her rain boots." He slid a napkin toward Milo; Wendy still had not wiped his face.

"A tip is a sign of appreciation. It's to show that you know the person behind the counter is more than just someone who's making seven bucks an hour."

"I'd like to be tipped," Pete said. Imagine that. What if his students tipped him for grading their papers or for holding office hours? What if he were tipped for what he was supposed to do?

"You make a decent salary," Wendy said.

"I work harder than that pincushion over there," Pete said, jutting his chin toward the boy behind the counter. "Do you know how many hours I spend a week writing comments that I know the students don't read on their papers?" Pete held a napkin out to Milo, who grabbed it and balled it up.

"Can you please, please, just try to enjoy your life for a few minutes here?" Wendy said.

No, Pete thought, sipping coffee that tasted charred and over-roasted and not at all like the lush vibrancy of the rainforest, he could not enjoy his life. He looked at the biscotti, wet and crumbling in Milo's mouth and pasty on his fingers, and thought, *My life is like soggy biscotti.*

When they got home that evening, Gary had already returned from work. He worked for a cell phone company doing something related to business, but Pete could not figure out precisely what Gary did. All he knew was, Gary made enough money that Wendy could work at home as a freelance graphic designer.

Gary sat on the couch with his laptop computer resting on the curve of his stomach. "Look, guys," he said, turning the computer around so they could see the screen. There was a man wearing a pink-and-green-striped shirt and blue plaid pants swinging a golf club on the screen. "It's my avatar. Do you think it looks like me? I've been building him for a few days now."

The man on the screen did, indeed, look like Gary. And like Milo. It was another member of their Kewpie doll army. Gary smiled at Pete and said, "I gave him a little more hair than I have. Wishful thinking, I guess."

Pete leaned over and examined the man on the screen. He was swinging his golf club through the air again and again. "You built him?"

"Yeah. I got to choose the nose and eyes and lips and ears and everything. It took me a while to build him, but it's taken me even longer to choose his clothes. I want everything right before I begin playing, you know?"

Pete nodded, but he had no idea why a grown man would waste so much time doing such a thing. Didn't people have things to *do* with their lives? This was the problem with the younger generation of men. They were so bored that they needed to inflict harm and pain on themselves, punch holes where they were not needed. Or, for those who were too soft for this sort of self-mutilation, there were computer games, which allowed young men to do on the computer what they should be out doing in real life.

"You spend too much time playing your games," Wendy said, and Pete restrained himself so he would not agree with her out loud. Wendy lifted the computer off Gary's lap, put it on the coffee table, and placed Milo in Gary's arms. "I'm going to make dinner now," Wendy said. "Don't get him too worked up. He needs to go to bed in an hour."

Gary nodded, but Pete didn't think Gary should let Wendy boss him around so much. He had never let his ex-wife, Laurie, tell him what to do, even when he knew she was right.

"It looks like it's just us guys here," Gary said to Milo after Wendy left the room.

"Indeed," said Pete. The three of them sat silently on the couch for a minute, Milo propped up on Gary's lap. All three stared at the TV against the other wall, although it was turned off.

What was Pete supposed to do with Gary and Milo? Without Wendy, their equilibrium was thrown off. He tried to think of activities they could all do together, and then he remembered what he had done with Wendy when Laurie had left them alone all those years ago.

"Wendy and I used to play a game called horsy. Her mother even bought us both cowboy hats," Pete said. "Stupid, though, since I was playing a horse and horses don't wear hats." Milo smiled up at Pete from Gary's lap. How were so many biscotti crumbs still stuck on his face and clothes? A sliver of pale belly poked out from underneath his purple T-shirt.

"We have cowboy hats," Gary said. "We got them from that ranch we went to in Montana before Milo was born. Hold on." He handed Milo to Pete and left the room. Pete brushed the crumbs off Milo's belly. He made sure Gary was actually gone and lifted Milo close and kissed his cheek. It felt soft, albeit sticky, and Pete settled Milo on his lap and poked his finger gently into Milo's cheek. Milo giggled, and Pete stuck his tongue out at him and crossed his eyes. Milo grabbed for Pete's mustache.

"Got them," Gary said, stepping back into the living room with a cowboy hat on his head and another in his hands. Pete quickly shifted his face into a blank expression; it would be mortifying if he was caught making silly faces at a baby. Gary put the hat on Milo's head, and it sank down to his shoulders. "You better wear it," he said, placing it on top of Pete's head. The gesture felt strangely intimate to Pete, another man putting a hat on his head, but there was nothing he could do to stop it.

"We'll have to find a smaller one for you," Pete said to Milo.

"Oh, I know," Gary said. "We should tie a bandana around his neck. That's sort of a cowboy thing, right?"

"I guess," said Pete.

Gary picked up a teddy bear that was propped on a recliner in the corner. The bear had been Wendy's when she was younger; now it was worn, and stuffing seeped out of one of its paws. Pete remembered that Wendy had brought it with her to college, and by the end of her freshman year, when Pete and Laurie had arrived to drive Wendy home, the bear had acquired a pink bandana tied around its head, babushka style.

Gary folded the bandana into a triangle and tied it around Milo's neck.

"It's pink," Pete said.

"We're trying to teach him that colors are non-gendered," Gary said. Then he shrugged. "It's one of Wendy's things. I think she read about this on some parenting blog."

"Do you agree with all that? That flowered carrying pouch, the purple shirts?" Pete said. All of this just seemed a way for Wendy to be difficult, for her to dare the world to question her parenting skills.

Gary shrugged. "I don't really mind the way he dresses and if he plays with dolls and stuff. As long as the kid's healthy, it's all good, right?"

This was the problem with Gary: he was too easy, too content. There was no fire in him. He was too agreeable. But Pete supposed a person had to be, in order to deal with Wendy. This had been the problem between him and Laurie. Both of them had loved a good fight, had argued for hours until their throats were sore and Pete had to teach his classes the next day with a lozenge wedged in his cheek. Fighting hadn't gotten him anywhere in his marriage, but, damn it, what fun was it to be so agreeable all the time?

"So what's this horsy game?" Gary said.

"Right." Pete stood up from his seat on the couch, then lowered his body onto all fours. He had to make sure to keep his head elevated so the hat didn't fall off his head. "Put the baby on my back." He wasn't sure this was such a good idea; after all, he was thirty years older than he had been the last time he'd tried this, but he was already on the ground, and he had no idea how else the three of them were going to pass the time before dinner.

"Are you sure it's safe?" Gary said.

"Of course it's safe!" Pete said. He felt a crackle of pain in his right hip, but he'd started this game, so he had to finish it no matter what. And what would happen if the baby fell off? The whole house was childproofed, no sharp corners anywhere, everything under lock, cushiony carpets covering the floors. "Do you know that Wendy never wore a helmet when she rode her bike as a child? And she survived."

"Helmets save lives," Gary said. "Seriously."

"You want to put a helmet on the baby?"

"Well, no, I guess not. He doesn't have one," Gary said. He lowered Milo onto Pete's back, settling the baby so he was on his belly, his arms clutching Pete's sides. After a few moments of wiggling, Milo was steady.

"Should I hold on to him?" Gary said.

"No, no, don't be silly. How's the boy going to grow into a real man if you're always holding his hand?"

"He's six months old."

"Just watch," Pete said. He began to move slowly, crawling on his hands and knees. He tried hard to keep himself steady. He didn't want Milo to fall, certainly, but he was also tired of the coddling Wendy insisted upon. A child needed to have some fun, and basil lemon sorbet and overpriced biscotti did not constitute fun. Pete began to neigh, making long horse whinnies, and soon enough Milo laughed that deep belly laugh, and Pete could feel the vibrations of laughter in his spine.

Gary pulled his cell phone out of the back pocket of his jeans and held it up, facing Pete and Milo. He followed them as they played horsy, Pete neighing and Milo chuckling, and Pete figured there was a camera in the phone and Gary was taking pictures to show to Wendy later to prove that sometimes it was OK to play without toys that were handcrafted in Germany or approved by the American Pediatrics Association. Sometimes it was OK to get your hands a little dirty.

It turned out to be a video, not photographs, that Gary had captured on his phone. This wouldn't have been so much of a problem had an unfortunate technological screwup not unfolded after Pete's return to school after Thanksgiving break. Wendy had sent an e-mail to Pete with a link to the video, which she'd uploaded to YouTube. However, she'd gotten Pete's e-mail address wrong. They almost never communicated by e-mail, and Wendy had made a mistake when she'd entered his e-mail address. She'd sent it to ppeterson@willard.edu, but that was Paul Peterson in the Philosophy Department's address. Since there were two P. Petersons on campus and Paul's name came first alphabetically, Pete's address was ppeterson1@willard.edu. The e-mail linked to a video posted on YouTube titled "Grandpa Pete Rides Again." The message in the e-mail read: "Proof that you're not as mean as you try to act. xoxo, Wendy."

Paul Peterson had forwarded Wendy's e-mail to the entire faculty, staff, and student distribution lists of Willard College. He'd written to Pete: "I believe this belongs to you, old buddy. xoxo, Paul." There was bad blood between Pete and Paul. During the Reagan administration, Paul had been the faculty advisor for the campus's Young Republicans club, and one day Pete had seen them gathered in a circle in a classroom nodding earnestly at some propaganda Paul was spewing. Pete couldn't help himself. He burst into the classroom and declared, "Young people who are Republicans are soulless! When you're old and rich, it's understandable, but you young kids have no fucking excuse! Save yourselves now!" Paul had stared angrily at Pete and pointed to the door and said only, "Out!" Since that incident, they'd kept far from each other. And now this.

The video had already been viewed 973 times. And there were comments below the video, pages and pages of them. One comment was from Cindy Martin, one of Pete's senior advisees. Her message read: "LOL, Professor Cowboy Peterson! OMG, his granddaughter is soooooo adorable!"

"Goddamn purple shirt," Pete said. He scrolled through the rest of the comments, clicked through all the pages, and most of them talked about how this didn't seem like the same man they saw in front of their classrooms. Someone named bananabrain12 wrote: "so this is what PP does when he's not circling clichés." Ida, the English Department's administrative coordinator, had commented, "We all knew that underneath it all, Pete is a marshmallow." George Winters, who used georgewinterstorm as his screenname, had written, "Prof must of been smoking the good shit."

How many people had seen this video already? And how many would view it later, after their classes let out, after band rehearsal was over, after they'd cleaned up athletic equipment from the fields? Pete had worked so hard for so many years to craft his image in a very particular way, and he didn't like how, in a forty-four-second fuzzy video clip, all of that had been ruined. He reached for the barrel of pretzels he always kept on his desk, unscrewed the red plastic cap, and began to eat angrily.

At twelve fifty, when his noon composition class was scheduled to end, Pete left his office and returned to his classroom. The tip jar sat on his desk. He was expecting mean notes, maybe some pennies, chewed gum. But instead something heart-stopping awaited him: there was money in the jar, some bills crumpled, some crisp. He thought of his students: earnest and eager to please. They had followed directions diligently, and they had given him money. Pete counted seventy-three dollars and fifty-nine cents in the jar.

He'd only slammed down the tip jar in an effort to rehabilitate his reputation as a curmudgeon; he wanted to do something awful so that students would say, "Can you believe it? Professor Peterson asked for tips!" He'd wanted word to spread about how terrible he was, how mean and unreasonable. He wanted this action to overshadow the softhearted gooeyness they had seen on the video.

"Hey, Pete, you done in here?"

He looked up and saw Tyler Wells, the new hire, who couldn't have been more than twenty-seven years old. Tyler held *Leaves of Grass* in his left hand. His class would start in a few minutes. He was wearing faded jeans and a polo shirt, and his blond hair was short and spiked. He looked like a character from the *Peanuts* comic strip. Pete knew

Tyler let students call him by his first name, and they flocked to his office just to chat with him about their lives, and he seemed fully and wholly confident in who he was, in his jeans and spiky hair, in his casualness. Pete was sure that Tyler in the classroom was very much the same as Tyler outside the classroom.

"Did you see the video?" Pete asked.

"I did. You're a star," Tyler said. "They're all buzzing about you in the hallways. It's so wonderful, the way you and your grandchild get along. You can tell there's a lot of love between the two of you."

Pete noted that Tyler had refrained from designating a sex for his grandchild. He had at least been in academia long enough to know to always be careful, to never assume anything, lest someone jump down your throat and call you a racist or a sexist or any other "ist" or "phobe" one could inadvertently become with a small slip of the tongue.

"You could tell that from forty seconds of blurry video?" Pete said.

Tyler nodded.

"Amazing," Pete said. He walked out of the classroom, holding the tip jar carefully, as if it contained something extremely valuable. He felt guilty—he'd return the money the next class period—but he felt useful too, worth something. There was a kindness and a goodness in his students; even when he'd made his ridiculous request for tips, they hadn't laughed at him.

Had he once possessed some of that kindness? After all, he'd come from a similar place, had grown up among miles of cornfields in Ohio, and in his youth had been wide-eyed and trusting and eager to experience the world. He thought of Wendy's money floating into all those tip jars in Chicago. Did Wendy understand something he did not about how people should be treated? Had he known these things before his marriage had fallen apart, before all those years of teaching wore him down?

Pete returned to his desk, set the pretzel barrel full of money down, and clicked on the link in the e-mail again. The video appeared on his computer's screen. It began to play, and he was shocked to notice that it was not only Milo who was laughing. He was laughing along with his grandson; in fact, what he was doing could be classified as giggling. Pete pressed the replay button when the video ended and watched again, looked at himself on his hands and knees, the cowboy hat slipping over his eyes, his small, laughing grandson on his back. He watched the video again and again, listened to his own laugher echoing Milo's, and thought he recognized something familiar in the image of himself on the screen, as if he were watching a video of someone he'd once known long ago.

Bread

You may have seen my ex-boyfriend, Lenny, on TV a few weeks ago. He was the skinny guy, tall too, wearing clunky unlaced black boots and a denim jacket with a painted skull on the back that his kid brother decorated for him, and he was tearing through grocery stores late at night squeezing the loaves of bread until they were twisted and unsellable. He did this for a few weeks before the supermarket managers caught on and informed the police who informed the newspeople. That first night on the news there were just the grainy images captured on supermarket surveillance, but once they caught him, two nights later, they showed his senior portrait from high school where he looked all scrubbed down and innocent, his wavy brown hair hardened with too much gel.

During his bread squeezing spree, Lenny insisted supermarkets didn't have surveillance cameras. "Lizzie," he said, "who's going to steal chicken thighs or a can of peas?" After the third week of bread squeezing, though, Ma and I were watching the local news and they showed the surveillance tapes of Lenny, who they called the Bread Bandit. The newscaster said, "The Bread Bandit has hit local stores twelve times in the last three weeks," and Ma said, "Hey, I know that jacket!" and I said, "No, Ma," but she got up all close to the TV, her nose almost touching the screen, and said, "Oh that's Lenny all right with that Satan jacket and untied shoelaces." I could hear the excitement in her voice because Ma had never liked Lenny, said he was going nowhere, and wanted a good excuse to break us up. Ma called the police. I stood next to her wanting to hack through the phone cord while she spelled out Lenny's name nice and slow.

The next night, after he'd been caught, Ma couldn't take her eyes off the news, flipping from channel to channel to see their coverage of Lenny's story, and after each report she shook her head and said, "Always knew the boy was a pervert," as if squeezing bread was something really dirty. And then she said I was forbidden to see him, saying she didn't want people seeing me riding in Lenny's ancient Civic and wondering what sort of Bonnie and Clyde shenanigans the two of us were up to. What kind of man was Lenny, she said, nineteen years old, two years out of high school already, a good two years older than me, and spending his nights squeezing bread? Two days after Ma squealed on him, Lenny was fired from his job driving a delivery truck for Calendelli's Breads, and the new joblessness only made Ma think of him as more of a loser.

It was Lenny's job that got him in the trouble in the first place, what with his learning about how the whole bread industry works. "There are these ties on the bread bags," Lenny told me, holding up five fingers. "Bread's delivered to stores five days a week, each day except for Wednesdays and Sundays. And each day has a different colored twist tie. Monday's blue and Tuesday's green and Thursday's red." By this point he'd folded down three fingers and he finished up by saying that Friday was white and Saturday yellow. "If you go in the store on Thursday and grab a bag with a white tie on it, you'll end up with bread from the Friday before, almost a week old."

Lenny said a lot of the stores in the area were keeping bread on the shelves far longer than they should, which was wrong. But short of buying up the old bread, all Lenny could think to do was ruin the old loaves so that no one else would buy them. On the first night, he took me with him to an open-all-night supermarket and said, "Start squeezing." But I just couldn't ruin all that bread because I knew the loaves Ma bought sometimes sat around for more than a week since there were just the two of us and we didn't go through bread that quickly and after a week the bread was still OK. If it tasted stale, we'd just toast it and make do. So I skulked down to the end of the aisle, stared at the orange juice containers as if deciding on pulp or no pulp, from concentrate or not, with calcium or with extra vitamin C were all life or death decisions. A few minutes later, Lenny shouted, "Let's go!" like he'd just robbed a bank. I looked at the bread shelves and there were so many beaten up loaves of bread, loaves that looked like drenched socks that you've worn all day in a storm and yanked off, all twisted and shapeless. We ran to the car and he drove quickly, right onto the highway. Then Lenny rolled down his window, let the breeze blow his hair back, and whooped loudly. And then, after he'd calmed down, he brought me home, and in the driveway he said, "Lizzie, we did some good tonight." I shook my head because I thought he was nuts.

A few days later, Lenny wanted to do it all again, said he'd found another supermarket that was selling old bread, and again he squeezed and I pretended to shop. Afterwards he said, "Lizzie, you've got to try it. It's so simple and yet there's this rush of power and you get the sense that one person really can make a difference."

"I don't know," I said. "Aren't the supermarkets losing money?"

"I do this for the people," Lenny said, all serious, his eyebrows pushed together.

And that's the thing: Lenny really believed in what he was doing, despite how stupid it was. I never explained his logic to Ma; it wouldn't have made any sense to her. And Lenny never did tell anyone that I was with him all those times. I guess I stayed far enough away and looked busy so no one noticed me. But Lenny could have easily gotten me in trouble too and I would've been stuck with two hundred hours of community service like he got, but he kept quiet. The last time I talked to him, he told me he'd stay away, that he respected Ma's wishes, and he didn't want to get me in any trouble.

The day after Ma ratted Lenny out, she slipped on a patch of ice outside the house. She hurt her back pretty good, but I didn't feel too bad for her because I suspected it was God's way of telling her she should've just minded her own business. It's been a month since she fell, and Ma's getting better, but she's not all the way there yet. Since she's at home all the time, she watches me like a hawk and makes sure I don't call Lenny or go out to see him. After her fall, she said that I had to go to the grocery store each week and pick up all that we needed, since she wasn't about to haul bags of food out of the car with her aching back.

So now at the supermarket I linger in the bread aisle, breathe in real deep, inhale that dark, yeasty smell, and think of Lenny and his quest to right the wrongs of the world in his own small way. I look at the bread—Ma always writes "One loaf whole wheat" on our list—and I run my hands over the smooth plastic packaging so gently that there isn't even a chance of denting the loaves. And then I check out the colored ties and look for the oldest loaf I can find, and that's the one I put in my cart. It's not something big I'm doing, I know that, it's something teeny tiny, but I tell myself that it's one loaf of old bread that someone else won't unknowingly take home, and I think Lenny would be proud of me.

....

Faulty Predictions

....

Hazel Stump and I were not friends. I moved in with her for practical reasons. The summer people who came to the High Country to escape the humidity and mosquitos in Florida had driven up real estate prices too much for either of us to afford living on our own. I found my room in her house through the classifieds in the *Mountain Times* three years ago. Both of our husbands were dead, and both of us had spent enough years in Boone that leaving and starting over elsewhere would be stupid. You didn't just start over at our age. Well, maybe that's not completely true. Most of my friends had moved away. Even though there was an influx of Floridians here, there was also an outflux of older folks who could no longer take the icy, wind-whipped winters in the mountains. But I stayed, dealt with the winters and dealt with Hazel. Hazel irritated me in many ways, but she had ideas, and sometimes those ideas translated into something to do. And I was always looking for something to fill my days.

On Halloween, Hazel and I shuffled to her battered Ford Focus, nearly tripping over the flat sheets from our beds. We drove down the mountain dressed as ghosts—Hazel draped in a pale pink sheet, I in one with faded daises. Hazel was certain a murder would occur that night at Mecklen College, and she wanted to prevent it. She had told me to make costumes so we could blend into the party we'd infiltrate that evening. She'd given me only half an hour to create the costumes, and in my rush, all I could produce were the ghost costumes, eyeholes hastily cut.

Hazel drove erratically down 321. An enormous black SUV with Florida plates zipped past us, and the driver honked when Hazel swerved. Hazel rolled down her window and shouted, "Floridiot!" I worried we'd get pulled over. And what would the police think looking at the two of us, short, round women in our seventies wearing bedsheets with eyeholes cut out like we were characters in *A Charlie Brown Halloween*?

"Maybe you should take the costume off for driving," I told Hazel as she skidded around a corner. "I think it's affecting your peripheral vision."

"I got the bow perfect," she said. "I'm not untying it and retying it again."

She'd knotted one of her husband Walter's old ties around her neck so the sheet wouldn't slip off. She'd tied the tie like a bow, with two big red loops that hung down limply. The whole thing looked ridiculous, but at least she'd found a use for one of Walter's ties. He'd been dead for five years, but she still had all his things stuffed in the hallway closet.

The eyeholes on my sheet migrated toward my right ear, and I had trouble breathing. I should have cut holes for our nostrils and mouths. I pulled my sheet off.

"We need to hurry when we get there. Better to keep your costume on," Hazel said.

"It's two hours to Charlotte," I said. "I'll have time to get recostumed." I folded the sheet and held it on my lap. I looked over at Hazel; she wasn't wearing glasses under her costume. "Are you wearing your contacts?" I asked.

"I got one in," she said.

"Where's the other one?"

"On the bathroom floor somewhere. Or maybe Millicent ate it."

Millicent was Hazel's cat, a fat tan number who had never liked me, even though in all my life I'd never had a cat not like me. Small things—pennies, hard candy, buttons—disappeared in our house all the time, and I was certain most of these items had taken up residence in Millicent's enormous, swaying belly.

"You lose depth perception if you don't have two eyes," I said. "You have no depth perception and no peripheral vision. What if a deer jumps out?"

"I'll sense it," she said. Then, as maybe a gesture of kindness to me, she slowed down. I watched the needle on the speedometer drop from 75 to 60.

Hazel believed she could sense a deer because she was psychic. Sometimes she called herself a medium. She said she started getting psychic messages after Walter died. She heard voices from beyond the grave, but they were random people, people she did not know. She got a book from the library about being a psychic and read it again and again. Then she got more books. Then she went to Chapel Hill and met with a group of women who claimed to be psychics, and they told her she had "the gift." The only reason she worked so hard at being a psychic was because she hoped to talk to Walter again. After a year of building up her psychic skills, she opened a shop downtown near the university and did readings for ten dollars. It was a big change from her job as the bookkeeper for the dermatology clinic, which she'd retired from a handful of years before. Most of her psychic shop clients were college girls who stumbled in drunk and giggling and asked about their love lives.

Hazel had a little success with her psychic predictions the second year we lived together. She correctly predicted the exact dates when we'd have snowfall that winter, predicted the final score of the Duke-UNC basketball game in January, and predicted that Timmy Bender, a senior at Appalachian State, would win a seat on the city council. In February, she predicted there would be a fire at the general store on King Street, but no one listened to her. She went to the police, and they nodded and said they'd look into it. She went to the newspaper.

They told her they could only write about things that had actually happened, not things someone suspected would happen in the future. One week later, lightning crackled onto the building and burned a charred hole right through the roof. Then people started to take notice of Hazel.

After an article about her appeared in the *Mountain Times*, some communications students decided to interview her for the school's radio station. Some mountain folk came from nearby towns, hopeful, with ten-dollar bills crumpled and warm, wanting to know whether they'd make good money that year. People seemed to believe in Hazel's abilities, although I did not because Hazel was just flat-out wrong so much of the time. I didn't know if it was possible for someone to be wrong about pretty much everything in life and still be right with psychic predictions.

Take for instance our neighbors, Darius and Antoine, two perfectly nice young men. It started with their cat. They moved into the neighborhood a few months after I did, and after they arrived, Hazel no longer let Millicent outside since she said the boys had a serval, not a cat, and she worried the serval would eat Millicent. So all day Millicent sat by the front door and whined to be let out, howling as if someone had stepped on her paw. I told Hazel that Millicent likely had ten pounds on Darius and Antoine's cat, but Hazel ignored me. "I saw on my news that rappers have been keeping servals as pets and some neighborhoods have had problems with the servals eating house pets."

When she said *her* news, she meant Fox News, which she had buzzing on the TV all day. When I'd first moved in, I tried to explain that those people were fearmongers. Hazel said I was too influenced by the liberal media and Fox News was good, truthful news. I learned then that it was useless to argue with Hazel. And if Hazel was a right-wing nutcase, that wasn't really my concern. I'd just let her believe what she believed and would continue to sweep the floor on Fridays and take out the trash on Sundays and wash the sinks on Tuesdays and life could go on smoothly. We didn't have to be friends. We were just housemates, that's all. Usually I ignored her ludicrous statements, let them hang in the air with no response, but this time I demanded to know why she thought Darius and Antoine were rappers.

"Why else would they have a serval?" she said.

"They don't have a serval. They have a spotted cat," I said.

"Servals are from Africa," Hazel said.

"Are you saying that Darius and Antoine are from Africa? Because they're black? They're from Greensboro."

"Well, you know," she said, but I wasn't going to let her off that easy.

"They graduated from App State last spring. Darius works in the Housing Office there. Antoine is a cook at Ruby Tuesday. I doubt they earn enough money at those jobs to purchase exotic animals."

"Well," said Hazel. "There are other ways to earn money that certain types of young men engage in." Then she left the room because I was certain she knew I was about to give her a lecture. I wanted to tell her that just because she'd spent so many years isolated in this town where nearly everyone was white—the students, the tourists, the locals—it didn't excuse that kind of backwards thinking.

But they were nice boys, and Hazel knew it, even if she didn't want to admit it. For a few months, my heart medication had been mistakenly delivered to Darius and Antoine's mailbox, and one of the boys always brought it over when we were home. They could have just left the medication on the stoop so they wouldn't have to speak to us, but they were decent enough to knock on the door and stand on the porch and talk for a few minutes. And I liked that, liked talking to young people, even if it was just a short chat. I missed that from when I worked in the nurse's office at the high school. So often the kids who came to the office weren't really sick, at least not in the bodily way. Some were lovelorn and some had shattered dreams when they hadn't gotten into the colleges they'd wanted, and I knew the stomachaches and headaches they complained of were really symptoms of heartaches. I liked talking to these kids and was happy to write them notes excusing them from class for the hour or two they spent in the office. Talking with Darius and Antoine reminded me of those times when I felt most useful.

The business with Darius and Antoine and rappers and servals wasn't the only unpleasantness between Hazel and me. Right around Thanksgiving of the first year I lived with her, I heard music and stomping in the living room late one night. I poked my head out of my bedroom. Hazel must have thought I was already asleep, because she was dancing. Her eyes were closed, and she waved her arms up and down, as if she were a big bird about to land in a swamp. An egret or something. Then she lifted her legs one at a time, like a dog that needed to pee. But the strangest part was what she was dancing to. It was a commercial jingle, and the lyrics went like this: "Winterzing gum makes you sing! Sing, sing, sing! Your teeth so white you glow at night! Sing, sing, sing!" It was a stupid song, but somehow Hazel had gotten this gum commercial on a loop on a tape and was singing along and dancing her weird bird/peeing dog dance, and I just couldn't stop staring. And then maybe Hazel sensed something, because she opened her eyes and stopped moving, but the tape kept going, "Sing, sing, sing!"

"I wasn't doing anything," Hazel said. She turned the tape off.

"I didn't think you were," I said. "I just wanted a glass of water."

"You should really knock when you come out of your room," she said. "We need to establish some ground rules."

"I'm not knocking when I leave my own room. It's not something a sane person does."

"Well, then," she said. "You should work on not sneaking up on people. It's not decent."

"You're not decent," I said, and trudged to the kitchen to get a glass of water I didn't even want.

About a month later I found a Christmas newsletter poking out of a Lands' End catalog in the pile of magazines and catalogs I planned to take out for recycling. I read the newsletter; it was from James Stump, his wife Yvonne, and their daughter Kelly. A small image at the top depicted a dark-haired teenager in a red dress posing in front of a Christmas tree. They lived near New York City and James worked in advertising. The letter mentioned the successful campaign he'd led for Winterzing gum. Yvonne volunteered at the town library and organized the women's book club. Kelly was waiting to hear back from the colleges she'd applied to and had just finished a winning season as the captain of the field hockey team at her school. They seemed like an ordinary family, nice, and the only possible connection to Hazel was the last name. Was James her son? She'd never mentioned a son. And she'd never mentioned a granddaughter. Was James Stump the reason Hazel had danced to the Winterzing commercial? I didn't know. I also didn't know whether Hazel had meant to save the Christmas newsletter or whether she was hiding it, even from herself. I reread that newsletter, committed it nearly to memory, slipped it back into the Lands' End catalog, then left the catalogs in their pile. If Hazel wanted to read the newsletter, it was waiting for her.

"Tell me again what you saw," I said to Hazel as we drove into Charlotte. It had turned dark during our drive, but it was a clear, star-filled night. We were only a few miles from the college. I was thankful we hadn't gotten into a crash, since Hazel had driven the whole way with only the one contact lens.

"It's not like a movie in my mind. How many times do I have to tell you?"

"But what do you know?" I didn't really believe a murderer was loose on Mecklen College's campus. I wasn't particularly worried or scared, but I knew that we'd stick out in our pathetic costumes. No one dressed as ghosts for Halloween anymore, especially not college students. When I saw the students from Appalachian State wandering King Street on Halloween, most of the girls were dressed as tramps.

"All I know is that there will be costumes. And a knife. That's it."

"And how will we stop things?"

"We'll figure it out when we see it."

I doubted we'd be able to stop anything, but I wasn't going to argue with Hazel. Plus, I was having an OK time. At home, I'd just be waiting for trick-or-treaters who never showed up because we didn't live in the nice neighborhood. By this time of night I would have eaten half the candy I'd bought.

We arrived at the college, and I wished we'd gotten here in the daylight so I could better admire it all. The campus was covered in trees, and there was a pond surrounded by weeping willows, and the dormitories looked like small castles. Ducks floated in the pond, and their quacks echoed through the quiet night. I thought about how much Larry would have loved this place. We had made it a habit to walk through college campuses wherever we traveled because they seemed like safe, beautiful small worlds full of knowledge and potential. When we'd first gotten married, Larry had harbored fantasies of one day becoming a college professor. He'd always been interested in learning as much as he could about World War II because his older brother, Hank, had died at Normandy. Larry kept an old black-and-white framed photograph of Hank on his nightstand in all the bedrooms we'd lived in. Hank was so young, permanently captured as that handsome, strong-jawed twenty-three-year-old. After I moved into Hazel's house, I slid that photo of Hank into the bottom drawer of my dresser. It seemed even sadder now, even more of a tragedy, that he'd gone so young. I couldn't let myself be haunted by two deaths—one so long ago and one recent—and looking at that old photograph of Hank in his uniform just reminded me of too much history.

Larry always said he wanted to better understand wars, understand why they had to happen and how they changed the course of things. He taught high school history but said if he worked at a college, he could teach classes that were focused on World War II instead of only spending the two weeks every December that were allotted for it in the high school curriculum. He could spend his summers traveling and researching and writing articles and books and maybe all of that would help him understand what had happened to Hank because, after all this time, he still couldn't make sense of it. In the years after our wedding, Larry slowly earned his master's degree at night, one class at a time, paid for by the school district. He kept saying that one day he'd go back for his doctorate. But then years passed and he kept teaching at the high school and I kept working as a school nurse and then, before we knew it, we were retired, all those years behind us. I'd had dreams myself, of going somewhere far away, helping on overseas medical trips, the kind where doctors perform surgeries on kids with cleft palates. I thought also about flying to foreign countries and bringing medicine and mosquito netting to combat malaria. But I never did go; Larry and I only left America twice, once when we went to the Bahamas and another time to London, but never to any of those countries where I could do something that would help someone.

Hazel pulled her car into an empty faculty lot and yanked up the parking brake. She got out of the car and barked, "Get your costume back on."

I pulled the sheet back on and held on to the sides so it wouldn't slip off. Hazel walked quickly, and I did my best to keep up, but it was difficult because of the arthritis in my knees. Hazel walked toward the music, a loud bass beat pumping out of a stone building at the center of campus. Dozens of students congregated outside. Just like at home in Boone, many of the girls were dressed in revealing costumes. There were scantily dressed cats, princesses, and what looked like a group of butterflies with sparkly wings. Boys were dressed as pirates and cowboys and skeletons and vampires. There were a few aliens in green masks who were of indeterminate gender. Many of the students held red plastic cups, and the air smelled like beer.

"Come on," Hazel said, flipping up the edge of her costume until a hand emerged. She grabbed onto my sheet and pulled me toward the door. She pushed past the students congregated outside, and I kept saying "sorry" and "excuse me" from under my sheet as we shoved through the crowd. At the door, a tall man with thick, muscled arms stood in front of Hazel. He wore a black T-shirt with the word SECURITY printed on it. "College ID?" he said. "Mecklen students only. You two students?"

Even with the sheets on, could we somehow pass for twenty-year-olds? It seemed impossible.

Hazel shook her head, and the man crossed his arms and seemed to grow bigger right in front of us. "Can't let you in without an ID," he said.

I wondered what Hazel's next move would be. Would she argue with him? Would she try to push past him? Would she unveil herself and hope he believed we were harmless enough to enter the room with thrumming music and flashing red and blue and green lights? But Hazel didn't argue or fight; instead, she turned and dragged me away.

When we were on the lawn, under a grove of trees and away from the crowd of students, I yanked off my sheet and said, "We came all the way out here and you give up like that?"

Hazel draped the sheet back on me. "This isn't the right place."

"We're supposed to be at another college?"

"We're supposed to be here. Just not at that party. I'm seeing a building that's shaped like the letter H. This isn't it."

"If I were a killer, I'd go to this party. Look how easy it would be," I said, sweeping a hand toward the campus center. "Most of them are already drunk."

"It's not the right place," Hazel said again. "Don't argue. Let's go."

"Where?" I said.

"Just follow me."

We walked on a paved path that cut across the middle of campus past a row of dormitories, one named Anderson, the next Harris, the next Wilson. "No, no, no," said Hazel as we walked past each one. I wished I could see her face so I could tell whether she was nervous or angry, whether she thought our mission was urgent. We passed the Gorton Science Building, and Hazel shook her head. "No," she said again.

"I have to use the facilities," I said. Hazel spun in a circle and pointed to a gray building across the lawn. A square sign outside the building said "Lancaster Hall." Above the door, the word "History" was carved in the stone. "The door's open," she said, and I followed her across the lawn. I half hoped the door would be locked, because I delighted in Hazel's faulty predictions. But I also half hoped she was correct because of the pressure on my bladder. We walked up the stairs of the history building, I pulled the handle, and the door swung open. "Hurry up," Hazel said. "The bathroom's down the hall and to the left."

Once again she was right. Maybe Hazel was just observant; maybe with her one good eye she'd noticed someone going into the building earlier and knew it was still unlocked. And maybe there were signs somewhere directing people to the women's room. I didn't want to believe Hazel had any sort of psychic powers, but sometimes she just seemed to know too much.

After I'd finished in the bathroom, I walked down a hallway filled with professors' offices, and I thought of how Larry would have loved to work here in an office with books lining the walls and a small chalkboard affixed outside the door for students to write messages. In the foyer, Hazel stood in front of a large bulletin board.

"Look," she said, a finger on a pink flyer. I stepped closer. The flyer advertised an art exhibition that would be held on campus in November in the Polk Art Building featuring the work of sophomore art majors. On the bottom of the flyer was a sketch of the art building. It was shaped like the letter H.

"Have you been to this campus before?" I asked.

"I've never been here," she said. "I've wanted to visit for a few years now. But that's not what this is about. We're going to the art building." She walked toward the exit.

I followed her out the door. "If there's truly a murderer on the loose, don't you think we should call the police?"

Hazel stopped walking and turned to me. "Remember what happened when I tried to tell people about the lightning? No one believed me. They thought I was crazy."

As we walked farther from the main quad, an eerie quietness settled over the campus. I could no longer hear the music throbbing out of the campus center, and I saw no students anywhere. I wondered why the college had decided to construct the art facilities so far out of the way. I didn't want to be in the cold, dark night anymore, my knees aching, charging toward an art building that might house a murderer. I longed for the dullness of Halloween at home, wanted to be sitting in my comfortable chair by the front door, a hand plunged deep into a plastic pumpkin filled with Reese's Peanut Butter Cups.

"Here," Hazel said, reaching out and taking my arm as if I were a blind person. "Don't trip." She led me over a wooden bridge covered in chipping red paint, and there was the Polk Art Building, a large concrete structure with light bleeding out from a side window. "Come on," she said, pulling me toward the lighted window. We walked through underbrush to the side of the building. The illuminated window was large, and we could see into the entire room. It was a studio, and only one person, a girl wearing paint-splattered overalls, was in it, painting. Her back was to us. "Keep your mouth shut," Hazel said, and led me right up to the window. When we got close, I could hear music playing in the room, something upbeat and cheerful. The girl dipped a paintbrush into a glass jar and cleaned it off.

"Is she in danger?" I whispered.

"What did I just tell you?" said Hazel. "Be quiet."

"If she's in danger, we might be in danger too," I said.

Hazel rubbed her temples, or what I assumed were her temples, through her ghost costume. "I might have been wrong," she whispered.

"Wrong?" I said. "What do you mean by 'wrong'?"

"I don't think there's a killer here."

"Then why are we here?"

"Just please, be quiet. Watch. Something is going to happen."

"Something bad?" I said.

"Just something."

"I'm taking my costume off," I said, and Hazel reached out and said, "No, please don't. I don't want to be the only ghost here."

We crouched, and my knees hurt. The girl moved her painting and the easel it rested on so it was under a bright lightbulb that hung out of a silver lamp strung from the ceiling. Now the painting faced us. It appeared to be a self-portrait. The girl in the painting had long brown hair and dark eyes and tan skin. I could see her features better on the painting than on her actual face. The painting was good, one of those pieces that's so realistic it looks almost like a photograph. The girl reminded me of the women I'd see on commercials and on the covers of brochures at the doctor's office; it was impossible to tell her ethnicity. I thought they used these actors and models in the commercials and brochures so everyone might see some of themselves in the women, might think they had some sort of connection. The girl could have any mixture of Spanish or Filipino or Eskimo or Hawaiian or Native American or Japanese or Chinese or Venezuelan or maybe even something Middle Eastern. She looked like everything at the same time and nothing specific; she looked like the face on the cover of my *Time* magazine when it had the headline "This Is What America Looks Like Now."

A new song came on inside, and the girl put down her paintbrush, looked around quickly, and when she confirmed that she was the only one in the room, began to dance. At first she was hesitant, but she got more and more bold, and her arms came out into the air, flapping like wings. She ducked and squatted and flapped. I'd seen this dance before.

"Kelly," I said. Even almost three years later, I remembered the name in the Christmas newsletter.

Hazel turned to me. "What?" she said.

"That's your granddaughter."

"Don't be foolish. I've never told you about a granddaughter."

"I'm turning psychic too," I said. "I know things." I tapped the side of my head.

"You know nothing," Hazel said, but she sounded puzzled.

"Let's go talk to her," I said.

"I don't know that girl," she said.

"And yet your intuition led you to her."

"Stop talking," Hazel hissed.

I tried to picture the Christmas newsletter I'd found tucked into the Lands' End catalog. I remembered the image of a dark-haired girl standing in front of a Christmas tree. "Why don't you ever talk about your son?" I said. "It's like he doesn't exist."

Hazel sighed. "We haven't talked in twenty-three years. And that's all you need to know."

"Is it because he married someone who wasn't white? Yvonne?" I felt like a detective attempting to solve the mystery of Hazel Stump. There was enough about the girl that reminded me of Hazel but there was also clearly something else mixed into the DNA.

"I'm not a bigot," Hazel said. She breathed in hard, and I saw the sheet over her nose pull in by her nostrils.

"Then why do you hate Darius and Antoine? They're nice boys."

"I just think they might be trouble," she said. "And I don't like that they brought a wild animal into the neighborhood."

If anything, Millicent was the wildest animal in the neighborhood, her yellow eyes glowing as she hissed and gurgled and howled for treats she did not deserve. The boys' spotted cat often came up to me when I walked to the mailbox and wound around my ankles, purring, begging me to pet it.

I didn't know what brought us here, whether Hazel had known Kelly attended Mecklen College, whether she'd known Kelly would be in the art studio instead of partying with her classmates. I didn't know whether at any point that night Hazel had actually believed there was a murderer on the loose, but now that we were here, there was something to be done. I thought about Larry and all those years he'd wished he could have become a history professor, about the books about the War he thought he'd write one day. I thought about my own desire to go overseas and help those who had little access to medical care. Now I could never do it; with my heart problems, it wouldn't be safe to attempt such a trip. But here was Kelly, and Hazel could easily go speak to her.

"Go," I said. "Take off the costume and go talk to her."

"What would I say?" she said.

"Just say hello. She's your family." Larry and I had never had children, and we'd both come from small families. Now that he was gone,

I had no one. If I'd had a granddaughter just a few feet away, I would have marched right up to her no matter what had happened in the past.

Hazel straightened. It looked like her mind was made up. I expected her to unknot Walter's tie, pull off the sheet, and walk inside. But I saw that the areas under the eyeholes of her costume were wet. Was she crying? "I have no idea what you're talking about," she said. "I don't know who this girl is."

"Of course you do. She's your granddaughter. She dances that ridiculous egret dance just like you. It must be genetic. No one else dances like that."

"I don't know what you're talking about. Maybe you have dementia," she said. Her voice cracked, and I could tell she was trying to be cruel so I would give up. "Let's go," she said. "I was wrong. No one is getting murdered here tonight. I just got a mixed-up signal."

"No," I said, and I stood behind her and wrapped my arms around her waist. I pushed her away from the window and toward the front of the building. "You're going to talk to her."

"Get your hands off me," Hazel said.

"I read a Christmas newsletter the first winter after I moved in. You'd left it in the living room. That's how I know about James and Kelly and Yvonne."

"I knew you weren't psychic! I knew you only knew things because you'd snooped." Hazel wiggled hard, her elbows poking at my arms, trying to escape. I linked my fingers together and held on as tightly as I could.

"Does he send you a newsletter every year?" I said. "Why would he send them if you don't speak to him?"

"He wants me to know that everything turned out OK. He wants me to know I was wrong."

"Maybe it's his way of reaching out to you. Maybe you should call him."

Hazel snorted and attempted another escape. I tried to push her forward, but she made herself heavy, spread her legs wide so she was firmly planted to the earth. Then she suddenly slipped from my grasp, whipped around, and pushed me to the ground. I landed on fallen leaves and small rocks, and I could feel the rocks scraping my back. Hazel's hands were on my shoulders, and she pushed me hard into the ground, and it occurred to me that this was the first time in my life that I had been in a fight. I wondered if she would punch me. I tried to move my arms, but Hazel's grip moved down to my biceps, and I was pinned.

A window slid open, and the girl inside the studio stuck her head out. "Who's there?" she said.

"Kelly?" I shouted.

Hazel moved one hand to cover my mouth, but she was still straddling me, the other arm across my upper chest now so I couldn't budge. I could barely breathe with her hand pushing the cloth of my costume onto my face. She leaned in close and whispered, "My boy, Jimmy, was a wrestler in high school. We were close then. I went to all his meets. He taught me moves."

"Who's out there?" Kelly yelled. "I already pressed the emergency call button in here, so security will be here in a minute."

Hazel and I scuffled, but I was pinned and Hazel's hand was still over my mouth.

"I can hear you. I have a knife," Kelly shouted. Her arm popped out of the window, and she held a large X-Acto knife in her fist. "I'll use it if I have to."

I wanted to tell Kelly not to be scared, that we were just two old ladies, one of us frail and pinned to the ground, the other related to her by blood. How wonderful it would be if Kelly could speak to Hazel, and then Hazel could see that this girl was pretty and talented and it was no matter at all that Kelly's skin and hair were dark because she was Hazel's granddaughter and what a waste it was for them to have never gotten to know each other. I stared up at Hazel and tried to see her eyes, but I could only see the holes cut into the sheet. I'd never really believed in Hazel's psychic abilities, but now I tried to wordlessly communicate with her, thinking, *Please, please say something to Kelly.*

Footsteps crunched over the dried leaves behind us. "All right, you two, get up." A campus security guard stood over us, his flashlight's beam shining down. He looked almost as young as Kelly, with unlined skin and a high and tight military-style haircut. Kelly slid the window open all the way, then stepped through it and jumped to the ground. She still held the X-Acto knife. I thought of Hazel's prediction about a knife and someone in costume and realized it had come true. "I said stand up, ghosties," the security guard barked. He held his walkie-talkie up and said, "10-20 Polk Art Building. Some drunk kids looking for private time in the woods."

Hazel let go of her grip on me and stood up. I tried to move, but my back hurt and my heart pounded and my knees felt locked. I needed help. I reached a hand up toward the security guard, but he said, "Haul your own ass up. Now!" I still had the sheet over me, and I realized he didn't know my age and thought I was a hooligan. Hazel reached over and took one hand and then the other and slowly pulled me up. When I stood, I hurt all over.

"Take those pathetic costumes off," the security guard said. Neither Hazel nor I moved, and the guard stepped toward us. "You want to take the costumes off yourselves, or you want me to do it for you?"

I took my sheet off and dropped it to the ground. "Oh," said the guard, staring at me.

"Oh," said Kelly. She stepped closer to us, her face revealing that she was more intrigued than afraid now.

"Now you," the guard said to Hazel, but his voice was gentler.

"I don't want to," said Hazel. But she reached up and unknotted Walter's tie and took the sheet off. She let it drop to the leaves and twigs by her feet and held only the tie. Her eyes were red, her hair mussed and sweaty. She draped the tie around her neck.

"What in the world?" said the security guard. "What were you two doing here?"

"Fighting," I said.

"Fighting?" said the guard. "You live in town? You need a ride home?" Now he was speaking to us as if we were deranged, as if we'd escaped from a mental institution. "Do you remember where you live?" he asked.

"We know where we live," I said. "We drove here."

Hazel stared at Kelly, who still stood holding the knife out.

"You know these two?" the guard said to Kelly.

Kelly shook her head. "I've never seen them before in my life."

I wanted Hazel to say something to Kelly, to tell her that she was her grandmother. I wanted her to give Kelly our phone number and to tell her that once she'd processed it all she should give us a call and maybe when she had a break from school she could come visit us. I wanted Hazel to clean out Walter's clothing from the closet in the hallway so Kelly could leave her things there, so she could stay a while when she visited.

The walkie-talkie crackled. "10-22 duck pond, Don. Skinny dippers," a voice on the other end said.

The young man sighed. He lifted the walkie-talkie and said, "10-4. Be there in a few. Need to escort two people off the premises first." He turned to the girl. "You should bring a friend with you when you work in the studio late." She nodded. "And you two, I'll drive you back to your car if you tell me where it is."

"You want to say anything?" I said to Hazel. She shook her head.

"I'm sorry we scared you," I said to the girl. "We didn't mean to. You're a really talented artist."

The girl didn't say anything, just looked at me like I was the strangest person in the world.

"How did you know my name?" she said. "You're the one who called out my name, right?"

"No," said Hazel. "We saw some girls walk by. They were dressed like cats. They called out to you. You're Kelly?"

The girl nodded. "It was probably my roommates. They wanted me to go to the party, but I still have a lot of work to do before the art exhibition."

"You're very industrious," I said. "An excellent trait in a young lady. I bet you're a good kid. A good, smart, hardworking young lady anyone would be proud to know."

"We need to go," Hazel said. Her eyes were still fixed on Kelly, who looked at me. I was certain Kelly was now convinced I was crazy.

"All right, into the back," said the security guard, and he led us to his car that looked like a cop car but said Mecklen College Security on the side. Hazel told the guard our car was parked in the faculty lot, and the guard asked if we were professors.

"Yes," I said. "We teach history."

Hazel looked at me as if I were insane, and I thought how much her expression looked like Kelly's.

"Actually," I said, "I left something in my office. Can you drop us off near Lancaster?"

Hazel shook her head, but she didn't say anything. She popped out of the car as soon as it stopped in front of Lancaster Hall.

"You want me to wait?" the security guard said. "I can drive you back to the faculty lot."

"We'll be fine," I said, and I got out of the car. I didn't hear the engine start, and when I turned back, I saw him watching us to make sure we'd get in the building OK, and I held my breath as I reached toward the door handle. If it was locked, our lie would be obvious. We didn't have keys. The door opened, though, and I let my breath out, and I turned and waved at the security guard, and he waved back and drove away.

"He was nice," I said to Hazel.

"You think everyone's nice. Him, that girl, Darius and Antoine. Everyone's your best friend."

We stood in the foyer, and right behind Hazel was the flyer for the art show. I wanted to take it, bring it home, hang it up on the refrigerator. Maybe Hazel would look at it each time she opened the refrigerator door, and maybe she'd somehow convince herself that it would be a good idea to go see Kelly's exhibition.

"Well, your granddaughter did seem like a nice girl."

"Did you see her?" Hazel said. "She was dark. She looked nothing like me. Or like Walter."

"She's your granddaughter. She danced just like you. You wanted to meet her. And then you chickened out."

"Stop," Hazel said. "Just stop talking."

"Why don't you speak to your son? Is it because he married Yvonne?"

"I don't have a son," Hazel said.

"Yes, you do. He taught you how to wrestle." I rubbed the back of my neck, which was still sore.

"I don't have a son. I have a house and a closet of Walter's clothes, and I have you. And that's all."

"Me?" I said. I thought I was nothing to her but an annoyance and someone who could be relied upon to write a rent check every month. But maybe Hazel was right about this one thing. We both carried ghosts with us—everyone our age did—but what was important in the day-to-day was who was there, who we shared a pot of coffee with each morning, who would make sure we didn't fall when we climbed on step stools to change lightbulbs, and who we said "good night" to every evening.

"Why'd you want to come back here?" Hazel said.

"I knew there was a bathroom here. It's a long trip home." I didn't tell her that I'd really wanted to come to pull the flyer about the art show off the bulletin board.

"You have a bladder the size of an acorn," Hazel said. "Well, go already," she said, pointing toward the bathroom.

When I emerged from the bathroom, Hazel was no longer in the hallway. I called out her name and heard only the echo of my voice. Beyond the foyer the halls were dark. I held my arms out in front of me, feeling for obstacles, and took tentative steps down the darkened hallway. Halloween cast its spell on the silent, empty building. This echoing hallway, probably so alive during the day, was exactly the type of place where ghosts might appear after the lights were shut off. I thought of how badly Hazel wanted to see Walter again, how all of this psychic business was so she could communicate with him, and although I would never admit it to her, I wanted the same thing. How nice if Larry could appear somehow in this darkened hallway. I imagined opening the door to one of the offices and seeing Larry behind a desk, his glasses slipping down the bridge of his nose as he read a thick book.

I heard a scratching sound and moved toward it, and when I got close enough, I saw that Hazel was at the end of the hallway. She held a piece of chalk and was writing on one of the chalkboards outside a professor's door. Then she moved to another chalkboard a few steps down the hall and wrote something else. I found the light switch on the wall and flipped it up, and the fluorescent lights flickered on. Hazel turned to me, blinked. She looked surprised to see me, as if she hadn't heard me moving toward her. Walter's tie was still draped around her neck.

I looked at the chalkboards outside the professors' offices. On three of the chalkboards, Hazel had written HS JS KS. "What are you doing?" I asked.

"Nothing," she said.

"What does HS JS KS stand for?" I said.

"Nothing," she said again.

I stared at the letters, as if they were one of those puzzles where all you had to do was rearrange the letters and then a word would emerge. "There are no vowels," I said.

"What're you talking about?" said Hazel.

"How can you form words with no vowels?" And then, as I kept staring, I understood what the letters were: they were initials. Hazel Stump. James Stump. Kelly Stump. Hazel couldn't allow herself to say anything to Kelly, but she could mark the chalkboards in a building at Kelly's school.

"Are you done with the bathroom? Are you ready to leave?" Hazel said. Her fingertips were covered in chalk dust.

"Finish up," I told her, and I watched as she put the initials on chalkboards outside of all the offices in Lancaster Hall. I stood in the quiet hallway and waited for Hazel as she spelled out the connections she could not bring herself to acknowledge in any other way.

A Good Brother

On Friday afternoon, Carter lovingly buckled his golf clubs in the backseat of his Jetta and drove from Philadelphia to his parents' house in Boston. He had little time to enjoy golf now that he was a medical resident, and he looked forward to his round the next morning. As he drove, he fantasized about his club coming in satisfying contact with the ball. He turned down the volume on the radio and talked out loud, pretending he was a professional announcer. In hushed tones he spoke of the fluidity and rhythm of his own hypothetical backswing, the almost impossible stillness of his head as the club moved through the ball and into the follow-through.

When he arrived at his parents' house late at night, his mother informed him that his Saturday morning golf plans had to be cancelled. Instead of playing golf, he was to take his sister wedding dress shopping; there was no one else who could do it.

The next morning, as his mother waited for her coffee to brew, she said, "You'll have to move your clubs so after you buy the dress it can be spread out in the backseat."

"The dress can go in the trunk," Carter said. He'd already reluctantly agreed to take his sister shopping. This felt like a large enough sacrifice. He opened a carton of almond milk, which his mother had bought especially for his visit, and poured it over a bowl of All-Bran.

Lacey, Carter's sister, hobbled to the counter—she'd broken her ankle tumbling off a scooter her numbskull fiancé had rented for a tour through the wineries of the Hudson River Valley—and took a glazed doughnut out of a box gaping open next to the sink. She rested her crutches against the counter, hopped to the kitchen table, and plunked down across from Carter. She took a large, sticky bite of doughnut. Carter fought the urge to tell her that she might cut back on the doughnuts if she didn't want to look like a puffed marshmallow in her wedding dress. Carter had inherited his mother's fast metabolism, but he was still fastidious about what he ate. Lacey was more like their father, short and round with a vicious sweet tooth.

"Your clubs can go in the trunk," Lacey said.

"I've got a bottle of wiper fluid in the trunk," Carter said. "Like I want that sloshing over my new Titleists."

"Oh, right, because I want my wedding dress to be dyed blue."

"Put the clubs in the garage," said Carter's father. "Case closed." Although Carter and Lacey were in their twenties, he spoke to them with the commanding tone he'd used when they were children. He swept a lint brush down the sleeves of his black suit jacket. Carter's parents were going to a funeral. Their neighbor, Elise McNamara, had died suddenly the week before from a stroke in the parking lot of her office complex.

Carter's mother shook her head. "You would think that on a day like today you'd be nicer to each other. Think about poor Duncan Mc-Namara. He's lost his mother."

"He's twenty-seven. He'll be OK," Carter said. This was probably not true. Carter had known Duncan since elementary school. Duncan had never had friends, and he was often seen around town with his mother, pushing her shopping cart at the grocery store, carrying her monogrammed canvas tote bag filled with books out of the library, even meeting her during his senior year of high school for lunch when he was allowed to leave school for fifty minutes. Duncan had spent time with his mother when other boys his age were practicing sports or driving too fast with their girlfriends in their passenger seats.

"Such a sweet young man," said Carter's mother. "And no one could have a better heart than his mother. She was holding a sweater drive for poor Guatemalan orphans."

"Don't poor Guatemalan orphans *make* sweaters? Like those hideous things made out of alpaca wool that they sell on the street for twenty bucks?" Carter said. He didn't want to talk about Elise's death and Duncan's loss.

"Can't you muster up some compassion?" said Carter's mother.

"I don't think Carter knows the definition of compassion," Lacey said.

"I know the *definition*. But if you choose to be compassionate to everyone all the time, you'll drive yourself crazy."

"This is the rhetoric of the uncompassionate," Lacey said. "And I think you're talking about Peruvians." She got up and hopped back to the doughnut box and helped herself to another doughnut, this one with a rainbow of sprinkles on top.

"Peruvian what?" said Carter.

"Peruvian alpaca sweaters."

Carter put a spoonful of cereal into his mouth and crunched loudly. It wasn't fair. This was the first weekend he'd had off since beginning his residency at Hahnemann. He had to finagle the entire weekend off—which meant he wouldn't have two days off in a row for the next three months—in order to come home for his father's sixtieth birthday celebration, which was to be held on Sunday. He dreaded the party. Relatives would swarm and say things like, "Your little sister's getting married. When's it going to be your turn?" He certainly didn't want to talk to his relatives about his love life. He'd had several brief relationships in the past, but mostly he liked to be left alone to do what he wanted. He didn't like people, didn't like dealing with their worries and concerns, and he certainly didn't want a girlfriend whose every need he'd be expected to attend to.

Carter had chosen radiology as his specialty because he wouldn't have to work closely with sad-eyed, hopeful patients, wouldn't have to break crushing diagnoses or hug jubilant patients who'd received a clean bill of health. He preferred x-rays, CAT scans, and MRIs to conversations and patient consultations. He worked nearly seventy hours a week, and after he was done working and going to the gym and cooking a healthy dinner, it was time to go to sleep, so there wasn't much time for socializing anyway.

But still, he didn't want to justify himself to loud, chatty relatives who'd talk with their mouths flapping open, spraying onion dip on his polo shirt, clamping fat, moist arms around his shoulders and booming out that they knew a nice girl and they could give him her number. But it would all be worth it because this day, this Saturday, he was supposed to play golf at the TPC Boston, a club Carter had never been to and would probably never have another chance to go to. Carter's acquaintance from high school, Josh, needed a fourth for his monthly golf game since their usual fourth, Mitchell Davenport, had strep throat, and Carter had readily agreed. He'd seen the rolling greens on TV, watched the Deutsche Bank Championship on Labor Day, and fantasized about reaching the second green in two shots, flying the wide lake that even Tiger Woods's ball had landed in.

But now everything was ruined. First, Elise McNamara had died and her funeral was scheduled for his golf day, so his parents could not take Lacey to get her dress. And Lacey had broken her right ankle; she couldn't drive herself and none of her friends were in town to accompany her. On top of everything else, the wedding dress couldn't be purchased at an ordinary store where Carter could slump in a chair and read magazines. Lacey was dragging him to something called the Running of the Brides at Filene's Basement.

What Carter knew about this event filled him with dread. Women lined up outside the store for hours before it opened and dashed inside as soon as the doors were unlocked and grabbed at highly discounted wedding dresses. Many wore bathing suits under their clothes so they could strip right in the middle of the room and try on dresses. It sounded barbaric.

"We're off now," said Carter's father. He waved, a look of stoic determination on his face, as if he were boarding a plane that would carry him to war. It was four hours before the funeral, but Carter's mother had a list of errands that had to be run before the birthday party the next day. She had to meet with the baker and the florist and the person inflating balloons to decorate the arch over the front door. Carter's father would serve as the chauffer for these missions, sit outside in the car and sip lukewarm convenience store coffee, listen to big band music on AM radio, and read a detective novel with the driver's seat tilted back while Carter's mother tended to matters inside the stores. Carter was sure his father did not care about the flowers at his party. He knew his father didn't have an opinion about whether the balloons should be sea foam or turquoise or cerulean, although his mother had spent forty minutes babbling about the merits of each color the night before while his father nodded over the sports section of the *Boston Globe*. In fact, Carter was certain his father didn't even want a party, but this was all to appease Carter's mother. And Carter knew his father agreed and went along with it because this was what married men did to keep the peace.

"You're driving too fast!" Lacey said. They were on their way to buy her dress, and Carter drove angrily. Lacey dramatically clutched the handle on the side of the passenger door. "Do you want to kill us?"

"Oh no," said Carter. "Don't order me around today. Save your bossiness for Rolf." Rolf was Lacey's fiancé. Carter had met him only three times but approached him with great skepticism. He was tiny, no more than five foot four, compact and dark haired, nothing remotely Rolf-like about him. Each time Carter had seen Rolf, he had been wearing a sweater vest. It was a strange uniform for a twenty-four-year-old. Rolf taught kindergarten, and Lacey had met him during her time in Teach For America in rural North Carolina. Now Rolf and Lacey both taught in a public school in the Bronx, which was filled with insolent children and run-down classrooms. Her job had created a small dent in Lacey's idealism, but she claimed it was Rolf who helped her get through this difficult teaching assignment. On the occasions when they'd encountered each other, Rolf had spoken to

Carter as if he were a young child, using more exclamation marks in his speech than any adult had a right to. "You're a doctor!" Rolf had said when they'd first met. "I better eat my apple a day when I know we're about to meet up!"

Lacey's hand reached for the steering wheel, and Carter batted it away. "You could stay in your own lane at least," Lacey said.

"I *am* in my own lane. Do you need your vision checked?"

"Just be careful." She turned her head and looked out the window.

"Do you think that bossy people naturally gravitate to teaching because they can be dictators over their classrooms?" Carter asked. He felt like annoying his sister, wanted her to feel the same level of irritation he felt about having to miss his golf game.

Lacey didn't answer.

"Is Rolf bossy too? He's got to be at least marginally bossy if he's a teacher."

"Rolf's a good guy."

"All good men wear sweater vests."

"I'm going to forgive your assholey behavior for today because I know you're upset about missing your golf game. And for that I'm sorry. But trust me, you weren't my first choice to accompany me."

"Why isn't Rolf here today?" Carter asked.

"Haven't you ever heard that it's bad luck for a groom to see his bride in her wedding dress before the big day?"

The big day. Of course Lacey would use an expression like that; it was the kind of phrase that would be splashed across the front of a glossy wedding magazine, circling the torso of a bride wearing too much bright pink lipstick.

There had been a time in Carter's life when he wasn't annoyed with everything about his sister. As children they'd made up games together, had schemed against their parents, trying to figure out ways to stay up past their bedtimes or watch television shows their parents did not want them to see. Carter remembered immensely enjoying one game they used to play. It made him feel daring and triumphant when they got away with doing slightly bad things. Carter liked this game because he was not, generally, daring. He had been the type of kid who would do his homework without being asked, who'd check over his math problems to make sure there were no mistakes, who would fastidiously clean his braces every night, surprising even his orthodontist with his thoroughness.

The game they'd played was called The Lie, and they would get themselves out of trouble by making up elaborate lies and delivering them to adults with straight faces. A library book that had been dropped in the bathtub turned into a book that got wet when they traveled down South for a weekend to build sandbag levees after a hurricane. A bike that Carter had left unchained at the park and was stolen became something he gave to the volunteers from the women's shelter who'd come to school to pick up boxes of donated winter coats. When Lacey had lost her dress shoes on picture day because she'd taken them off to jump in puddles in the school's playground, they told their parents that Lacey had given the shoes to a program called Shoes Across America, and people from the Museum of Fine Arts had come to school and collected a pair of shoes in every shape, size, and color for an exhibition on American footwear. In solidarity, Carter had hidden away his own dress shoes and claimed that he, too, had donated them.

"Remember The Lie?" Carter asked.

"Of course. I remember you were pretty much only nice to me when we were being lying degenerates," Lacey said.

He was taken aback. He'd been nice to Lacey at other times, surely. It wasn't fair of her to say that to him, and so it was his turn to retaliate with something unfair of his own.

"So . . . is your ankle really broken?" Carter said.

"No, it's fine. This is all a big lie and Mom and Dad are in on it. Elise McNamara? Not dead. Mom and Dad are just pretending to go to the funeral. And Mom's Subaru? Not in the shop. Dad hid it in the woods just so that you'd have to move your clubs from the backseat of your car. I hired a doctor to put this cast on. Because, as you know, doctors have nothing better to do."

Carter raised his hands from the wheel in a sign of surrender. "All right, all right. Sorry."

"Whatever." Lacey turned again to stare out the window. "Maybe we can get back in time for you to play in the afternoon at your fancy club."

Carter did not tell her that by the time they got home it'd be too late. They would be on the back nine by then, and he couldn't just trample through the course and announce he was ready to start halfway through. And so he said nothing, and they traveled the rest of the way to Filene's Basement in silence.

They parked the car in a lot and made their way to the line snaking in front of the store. Carter had never seen so many women gathered in one place. Most women appeared with a pack of helpers, and many of these groups had uniforms, sweatshirts with things like "Team Jody!" or "Walkowski Warriors!" sprawled across them in iron-on letters.

Some women in the crowd held up homemade signs with their dress sizes and the types of dresses they were looking for—A-line, empire, high neckline—scrawled on them in marker. A group of four noisy women, tough-looking and with thick arms, as if they'd spent their lives baling hay, wore headbands with antennas topped by glittery red hearts.

"What's that about?" Carter whispered, nodding toward the head-banded women.

"It's so they can find each other in the crowd."

Carter surveyed the throbbing crowd. Some women were pressed up against the door trying to peer inside. He thought about where he could have been at that moment, bending down to insert his tee into the lush, perfectly manicured grass of the first hole at the TPC. He imagined his driver cutting through the air, quick and smooth, and he pictured his ball carrying the sand and fading right into the middle of the fairway. The other players would suck in their breath in awe.

"Look," said Lacey, shifting on her crutches, "I know you don't want to be here. So thanks."

Carter shrugged. He didn't do well with gratitude, never knew what to say in return.

"I need your help inside," Lacey said. "I'm not going to be able to keep up with the crowd with my leg like this. You'll have to grab dresses for me." Lacey reached into her purse and took out pages ripped from magazines. "These are the kinds of dresses I like. Just simple. Not frilly." She smoothed the pages and handed them to Carter.

He flipped through them, then shook his head. "They all look the same."

"No, look," Lacey said, taking the pages out of Carter's hands and holding them up close, next to his face. "Sear these images into your brain."

"They're wedding dresses. It'd be like me giving you photos of twenty golf clubs and asking you to differentiate."

Lacey sighed and shoved the papers back into her purse.

"All right, all right. Give me the pictures." He looked and she was right, there were some subtle differences between the dresses, but they were still all big white dresses. "Got it," Carter said, handing the pictures back to Lacey.

"I want a dress with simple lines, OK?"

"Simple lines," Carter repeated. He wished she would stop talking, that this day would be over already.

"My dream would be a Vera Wang, but I'm trying to be realistic here."

"OK, Vera Wang," Carter said, nodding. He was just repeating words now; he had no idea who or what a Vera Wang was.

"Just look for something like the ones in the pictures," Lacey said.

"What size?" Carter said.

"What?" Lacey said, straightening so her crutches were perpendicular to the ground, her hands gripping the cushioned handles hard. She looked like an animal in defense mode, as if she might raise a crutch and swipe it across the side of Carter's head.

"What size dress do you need?" Carter said, pausing between each word, as if Lacey did not understand English.

Lacey stared at him and said nothing for a few seconds.

"What?" Carter said. He didn't understand why Lacey was upset. He hadn't been trying to goad her as he'd been doing in the car. He was asking a simple, easily answered question.

"I don't want to tell you," she said. There was a vulnerability in her voice that Carter found crushing. It took him back to when they were children, when Lacey was even shorter and rounder than she was now. He remembered the taunts on the playground, remembered the fat jokes, remembered Lacey crying about gym class and the cruelty she was subjected to during games of playground kickball when she ran so slowly that her team would always get out whenever she was up. And he remembered how at those times he'd boil, but what could he do? Back then he'd been thin and weak, and if he tried to stick up for his sister, he'd only get beaten up himself. Or he'd end up having to eat lunch with pathetic, friendless Duncan McNamara, and he'd have to listen to Duncan talk about all the fun he'd had with his parents over the weekend. So Carter would slink away from the taunts, and he'd be surly and quiet for the rest of the day. It was on those days that he'd try to make up for the other children's cruelty, when he'd try to be extra nice to his sister in small ways, letting her watch what she wanted on TV and helping her with her homework, but he always felt like a failure for not telling everyone to shut up. And now she was afraid to tell him her size. It was clear that Lacey didn't differentiate between him and the playground bullies from fifteen years ago.

Lacey shifted on her crutches and stood on her good leg. "I know how you are," she said, still unable to look at Carter, scanning the crowd instead of letting her eyes rest on him. "I know you think girls my size are barely human. I know it's all about flat stomachs and healthy eating for you. I just can't tell you my size."

"You'll still be the same size whether you tell it to me or not." He wanted to say the right thing, but it was impossible to know what that would be.

"I just don't want you to know," Lacey said quietly.

"Then how do you expect me to find you a dress?"

"No one looks at sizes anyway. Just approximate."

Before Carter could say anything more, the doors opened and the women surged forward and Carter was swept into the commotion of the crowd.

Once they were inside, Carter stood dazed. He wished he could make all the noisy, shrieking women in the room disappear. There were dresses everywhere, and greedy hands flew through the air. Everything was moving so quickly, and Carter felt like he was in the middle of an athletic event whose rules had never been explained to him. All around him, women were shedding clothes and pulling dresses over their heads and tossing crumpled rejects to the ground.

"Carter!" Lacey said, poking him in the calf with one of her crutches. "Move!"

Carter jogged toward a rack of dresses with the fewest women surrounding it, but in the seconds it had taken him to cross the room, the rack had been stripped bare. He bent down and sifted through the dresses that piled at his feet, loading them into his arms.

Lacey made her way over to him, and he held the dresses out toward her. She picked the first dress off the top of the pile. It was tiny, as if it were meant for a little girl. She let the dress drop to the floor. The second dress was far too big. The third was covered in ruffles.

"Did you even look at the pictures?" Lacey said, shaking her head. She pawed through the rest of the dresses in Carter's pile and dropped each rejected dress to the floor. "People have already grabbed the good ones. We should just go home. I knew this was a bad idea."

Carter looked over Lacey's shoulder and saw the group of women with the heart-shaped antennas. One woman, the shortest, held up a simple dress with thin straps. It looked like one of the dresses in Lacey's photos. Most important, though, it looked as if it might fit Lacey.

"Look," Carter said, pointing.

Lacey turned around. "That's nice," she said.

"You think there's another one like it here?"

They looked at the madness that swirled around them. More

dresses were mounding on the floor, stripped off and turned inside out. People were pushing, shoving, grabbing.

Lacey sighed. "If there is, we won't be able to find it."

The woman holding the simple dress took off a blue fleece jacket and pulled the dress over a tank top. She then took off her jeans under the dress and handed them to another woman in her group.

"I bet she'll buy it," Lacey said. "It's beautiful."

"I'll get it for you," Carter said.

"How do you think you'll do that?"

"I'll ask them nicely."

"You know nothing about human interaction, do you?"

But Carter was determined; the dress, he hoped, would help atone for the things he had done wrong, for the times when he hadn't stood up for his sister. He jogged over to the women, leaving Lacey to hobble her way through the crowd. When he reached the women, the short one handed her headband to an older woman. The woman in the dress piled her hair on top of her head. "I'm doing my hair like this. But, you know, nice. Like with flowers in it."

Carter extended a hand. "Hello. I'm Carter."

"You think this is a pickup joint?" the woman said, letting her hair drop loose. She did not shake Carter's hand. "I'm spoken for," she said, holding up her left hand to show Carter a blue gem the size of a large grape. She gnawed on a wad of fluorescent yellow gum, opening her mouth wide enough that Carter wondered if the gum might tumble out. The idea that she was the type of woman Carter would be interested in was preposterous.

"*I* just wanted to introduce myself because I need that dress."

"You a drag queen?" said one of the other antennaed women, letting her eyes roam from the top of Carter's head to his toes. She had a mass of curly blond hair, and her bangs were sprayed into a hardened wave.

"I don't actually need the dress. She does," Carter said, pointing to Lacey, who was still making her way through piles of dresses and packs of disrobing women. "Please, what are your names?"

The short woman stared at him through narrowed eyes. "I'm Kiki. This is my momma and these are my cousins, Marie and Joy. And this is my dress."

"Good to meet you all," Carter said, giving them what he believed to be his most charming smile. The four women stared back at him, uncharmed. The mother held the huge pile of dresses closer to her chest.

"You're in our way," said Marie.

"I just need that dress. Please." He tried to meet her eyes, tried to communicate desperation and sincerity, but Kiki turned and stared at her own reflection in a mirror. She spun and the skirt billowed out. The women admired Kiki and acted as if they hadn't heard Carter.

"You look sexy," said Kiki's mom.

"A bride shouldn't look sexy," Carter said, then bit his lip. He would need to watch what he said if he wanted to convince the women to turn the dress over to him.

"He's kind of cute, even though you can tell he's uptight," said Joy, smiling widely at Carter. She was missing a front tooth. Carter forced himself to smile back.

Marie punched Joy on the shoulder. "You ain't here to find a boyfriend."

Carter took out his wallet and counted the cash inside. "Look, I'll give you three hundred dollars for that dress."

Kiki laughed. "This dress is worth three *thousand* dollars. That's why it's a bargain. It's only going to cost me two hundred dollars."

Carter put his wallet away.

Lacey had nearly reached them, and he'd gotten nowhere. He had an idea, and his heart beat hard just thinking about it. He wasn't the type of person who ever lied to get what he wanted—even in childhood, The Lie was only used to get him out of trouble—but it seemed that there was no other way to accomplish what he needed to do. "That girl," he said, pointing to Lacey, "she's been through a lot."

"Oh yeah?" said Kiki roughly. She stared at herself in the mirror and smoothed out the wrinkles in the dress. "I been through a lot too."

"I mean *a lot*," Carter said. All those lies they'd told as children seemed like training for this one important event, the Olympics of lying. "Have you ladies ever heard of Russian mail order brides?"

Their gum stopped snapping. He'd gotten their attention.

"Oooh, I just saw this one episode of *Law & Order: SVU* where they had these mail order brides," Joy said. Carter tensed. He too had seen that episode just the week before, while he was running on the treadmill at the gym, and he had hoped to draw on the show for inspiration. He'd have to be more creative. "These bad guys," Joy continued, "they kept the Russian ladies in this basement and—"

"Shut up, dumbass," said Marie. "I want to hear his story."

By this time Lacey had made her way over to the group. "This is Yelena," he said. Lacey opened her eyes wide in surprise. Carter lifted his eyebrows, trying to let Lacey know she had to play along. "Come here, Yelena," he said, waving for her to come closer. "She hardly speaks English," he said, more for Lacey's benefit than for Kiki and her family. "So don't be offended if she says nothing to you. She's very shy, too." Lacey hung her head, playing along.

"So what are you, like, her pimp?" said Kiki.

"No!" Carter said, finding himself inexplicably offended.

"He's not dressed like a pimp," said Joy, eyeing him, taking in his J. Crew argyle sweater, khakis, and Sperry Top-Siders. "He dresses kind of rich."

"Stupid, pimps *are* rich," said Marie.

"Shut up, all of you," said the mother. "Tell your story." She was staring at him with wide green eyes and breathing heavily through her open mouth, and Carter could imagine her sprawled on a floral couch, watching soap operas with the same expression.

Carter knew he had to come up with something that would cause the women to feel sympathy. He'd have to figure out a story that was at least as interesting as an episode of *Law & Order*.

"I'm Yelena's English as a Second Language teacher. She's only been in the country for three weeks, brought over by this guy who's going to marry her. And of course no one wants to be a mail order bride, but what were Yelena's options?"

"Why?" said Kiki. "What was wrong with her life in Russia?"

Carter took a deep breath and said, "She made her living as a dog breeder, specifically Siberian huskies, but then one dog was infected with rabies and became insane and attacked her leg and she's had to endure many, many expensive surgeries, and she can no longer chase after the dogs, and if she doesn't get more medical care, she might never walk right again."

Carter could see he had all four women's attention; they were staring at him, waiting for more. "After the one dog got sick, the rest of her dogs got sick too and had to be put down and she was deeply in debt. A rich doctor brought her to America and promised to fix her leg and help her set up a new dog breeding business after she married him. She didn't want to come, but what choice did she have? Think how happy you'll make this poor woman if you give her that dress."

Lacey looked up at Carter and smiled.

"How'd you know about the dogs and all if she can't speak English?" Marie said.

"We have a translator at school."

"Why are you taking her shopping?" said Kiki. "Why isn't she with her man?"

"Don't you know?" Carter said. "The husband can't see the bride in her wedding dress before they get married. It's bad luck." He saw Lacey stifle a giggle.

"So you're just Mr. Nice Guy and you say, 'I'll take you dress shopping and then later, before you get married, there better be something in it for me, Miss Mail Order Bride'?" Kiki said.

"Oh no, no," Carter said. He was getting that rush he had experienced as a kid when one of his parents fell for a lie. "I just want to help Yelena. Let her have that dress so she can have one beautiful, unforgettable day."

Kiki put her jeans back on and pulled the dress over her head. "Here, stand up straight," she said, and tapped Lacey on the shoulder. Lacey straightened, and Kiki held the dress against Lacey's body. "Yeah, it'd fit her."

"She don't look as sexy as you," said the mother.

"You've got all these other dresses!" Carter said.

"But you want this one, Kiki," said the mother. "It's my favorite."

"If you give her this dress," Carter said, "you'll make her dreams come true." He sounded horrifically cheesy, using the type of phrase he'd normally cringe at, but he needed the dress.

"So, like, you know her real good and all?" Kiki said, staring hard into Carter's eyes. "Like you're her friend and you won't try to take advantage of her?"

"I'm her best friend in this country," Carter said.

"OK then, Mister Teacher, you tell me one thing," Kiki said.

"Anything."

"What's her last name?"

Carter paused. He couldn't think of anything that sounded right, and his mind plunged back to eighth grade World History. Finally, he spoke: "Gorbachev."

Kiki narrowed her eyes. "You think I'm stupid?"

"No, no, no, no," Carter sputtered. "I just couldn't remember it for a minute."

"You talking about that man with that red thing on his head? He's real famous. You think we're too dumb to know who that is?" Kiki's mother said.

"You're just like every other man, even with your nice clothes. I don't know what you're doing, but I know you're a liar," Kiki said, a finger pointing toward his face.

How had he let this happen? He'd been doing so well, had them all eagerly awaiting the next part of his story.

"Get away!" shouted the mother, and Marie pushed Carter so hard he fell to the floor. Joy squatted and offered him a hand. She grinned her missing tooth smile. Carter pushed himself up.

"Let's get out of here," said Lacey.

"Oooh, listen, she speaks good English!" Marie said.

Carter lunged at Kiki and tried to grab the dress. Marie reached out in an attempt to protect Kiki, and a long purple fingernail scratched Carter's cheek. He touched his face; she'd drawn blood.

"Liars!" Kiki shouted, clutching the dress tightly to her chest.

The mother pelted them with the wedding dresses she'd stockpiled, and Carter took Lacey's arm and helped her maneuver her way out of the store as Kiki and her family screamed insults at their backs.

As they drove home, Lacey hummed softly, although the radio was not on. From the corner of his eye, Carter saw Lacey tapping her fingers against the door handle in a steady rhythm, as if they were just out for a drive and nothing bad had happened.

Lacey's cell phone rang and she answered it. It was Rolf. She told him everything that had happened. "It's OK, though," she said. "Don't worry about it, baby. I'll get a dress somewhere else. And it was totally worth it. Carter went like all *West Side Story* on them, ready to rumble for me. You should have seen it!"

She played up Carter's braveness. She described the women as bigger and tougher than they were and told Rolf that Carter had left the fight with a bloodied cheek and he'd probably need a tetanus shot. "He was a hero!" Lacey exclaimed, and Carter felt surprise wash over him. No one had ever said such a thing about him. "Hey," Lacey said, turning to Carter, "Rolf wants me to tell you that you're a good brother."

"OK, thanks, I guess," Carter said.

"Rolf says one day we're going to tell our kids all about how Uncle Carter fought for a wedding dress for Mommy."

"OK," Carter said. Rolf was sappy and sentimental, but this was the way Lacey and Rolf were, overflowing with compliments. Mostly it was too much for Carter to handle, but this time he felt good, maybe better than he would have felt playing golf. He knew his golf fantasies would never coalesce into reality—he'd never make that shot Tiger Woods had missed; his ball would land right in the water with an unsatisfying plunk, and he'd be angry, digging the spikes of his shoes into the pristine grass, uprooting patches of turf.

Lacey kept talking, blathering endlessly to Rolf, and Carter thought that Rolf had to be enormously patient to put up with her. But this was what people did. He thought of his father in the parked car, watching through the window of the bakery as Carter's mother picked out the perfect birthday cake. He pictured Kiki carefully selecting those heart antenna headbands at the mall and presenting them to her family, slipping them on each woman's head early that morning. He imagined Duncan McNamara, sitting in the front pew at the church, trying not to cry as his father delivered the eulogy.

Carter slipped his hand into his coat pocket and felt his cell phone, cool, smooth as a stone, and quiet. He wanted to tell the story about lying to Kiki and the dress and the Siberian huskies and Gorbachev and the cut on his cheek. He wanted to talk about this morning in vivid, excruciating detail. Lacey giggled into her phone, and Carter took his hand out of his pocket, gripped the wheel tightly, and wished he had someone to call.

Miller Duskman's Mistakes

Miller Duskman's first mistake was shipping the fancy pizza oven from Italy to Morningstar, Ohio. His second was taking out a full-page ad in the *Star Record* to inform us that his pizza was made from a gourmet Neapolitan recipe. No one wanted his pizza with that burnt thin crust and the cheese made from buffalo milk. Why would anyone want anything to do with Italian buffalos when you could drive five miles from town and find farm after farm with cows producing good, clean American milk? If Miller had done his research, he would have known that in Morningstar we liked our pizza from Joe's, and we liked the crust doughy and thick, the cheese a gooey mix of provolone and mozzarella. We didn't need to see dough tossed in the air. We loved watching Joe push out dough with his stubby fingers in the dented metal pans he'd used for years. And besides, we had no money for twenty-dollar pizzas that wouldn't fill our stomachs. The glass factory had closed down two years before and the broom factory had closed right after that; many people were still out of work when Miller showed up.

I've run the Ladybug Bed and Breakfast for the last twenty-five years in Morningstar. Ask me anything about this town and I can likely give you an answer; people talk to me, tell me things. They stop by for a muffin or a cup of coffee—and mind you, I never charge anyone I know for food—and they tell me what they've seen and heard. And so when Missy Carlton, the librarian, stopped by with the newest Mary Higgins

Clark I'd requested, sipped the mug of Earl Grey with cream I'd prepared for her, and said there was a new face in town, I listened hard.

The rumor was that Miller had an aunt and uncle who'd lived in
Morningstar years ago, and he'd come to stay with them one summer
when he was a child. After he'd grown up and made his money on Wall
Street, he decided to come back to Morningstar because of his good
memories of that childhood summer. But I'm not sure if that story is
true. Miller couldn't have been older than thirty. Most of us have been
in Morningstar all our lives, and if a new child, especially one like
Miller with a head the shape of a tire swing, appeared for a summer,
we would have noticed. And there are no Duskmans in town, never
have been. Certainly no one claimed him when he showed up and
opened the Brilliance Café on Friendsville Street in the space where
Ike's Hardware used to be before Lowe's came to the north end of town
and drove poor Ike Bell into the grave. Even those of us who wanted to
keep shopping at Ike's had a hard time, since Lowe's was cheaper and
had a better selection. We wondered if the stress of losing his business
caused Ike's heart attack. We felt sorry about that, guilty, and swore
we'd do better about supporting our own.

Miller Duskman's third mistake was building the outside of the
Brilliance Café completely out of glass. Who wanted to be watched
while eating, like an animal in the zoo? I guess he thought it made the
place look cold and modern, like something you'd see in a city. All that
old brick and stone downtown, and then the Brilliance Café glowing
like some giant ice cube plopped in the middle of the block. I'm not
sure how the whole building managed to stay upright; I couldn't see
any metal or glue or anything else holding all that glass together. I'm
sure he got some architect from New York City to draw up the plans
for it, someone who knew nothing about the weather in Ohio, and I
didn't trust that the building would stay standing through the windy
fall and the blizzards of winter. Every time a storm hit Morningstar,
I'd wonder if the building would be knocked over in a gust of wind,
and I was always surprised when I drove by it and saw that it was still
there. To tell you the truth, that all-glass building was like something

magical, and maybe if someone we liked had constructed it, we would have been impressed. But we couldn't believe Miller tore down Ike's Hardware. The structure was sound, the floors made of good black cherry, and the building had years of life left. We watched the trucks from Lowe's deliver sheet after sheet of thick glass. Glass had once been manufactured in Morningstar, and as I watched the men unload the trucks, I thought about the time when our town was busy and people had good, steady jobs.

Construction on the Brilliance Café went on through the spring, and it opened on the first of May. The only people who went were the Lake College kids, checking it out before heading home for the summer. Of course the college kids ate there. They're not really from Morningstar; they're like the tourists who come for the Harvest Festival, except they stick around for four years. Word is Miller put an ad in the *Lake's Voice*, the paper at the college, with a coupon for 30 percent off any pizza. The kids piled in with that coupon and paid with their parents' money. Miller was a newcomer, an outsider, and all his business from Lake College just seemed to prove how much he didn't belong.

Once May ended and the students left, the Brilliance Café suffered. The only customers were the people who worked at the college. I knew Miller had to be thankful for the college's business; I understood how the college could keep a place afloat in Morningstar. Without the parents and the campus visitors staying at the Ladybug Bed and Breakfast, my business would be slim. But there was one crucial difference between Miller and me: my family has been in Morningstar for generations. My grandparents opened the bed and breakfast in 1927. No one in town faulted me when most of my business came from the college. And I provided a place to stay for those overflow relatives at Thanksgiving and Christmas that just couldn't fit into overcrowded houses—at a discount, always, for people I knew. In fact, I barely made a profit off any of the townsfolk. The outsiders were another matter; they were willing to pay far more than the rates at the Holiday Inn in Akron or Cleveland in order to absorb the charm of small town Ohio.

If they were lucky, they might even see one of the Amish buggies roll-ing by slowly in front of the B&B.

Sometimes tourists wandered into the Brilliance Café; maybe it re-minded them of home, of the types of restaurants they'd go to in their cities. But most everyone who lived in Morningstar made an effort to steer clear of it. When we saw Miller in town, we didn't say hello. We ignored him or gave him cold looks. And maybe Miller would have given up after a few months, packed up and moved back East, but then Avery Swenson returned. She'd just graduated from Ohio State, had her teaching degree, and everyone thought she would leave Morn-ingstar behind, escape the hurt that'd happened to her here. We were overjoyed when we heard she had signed a contract to teach third grade at Morningstar Elementary. Avery was a girl with options, and she'd chosen to come home.

When Avery was four, a semi from Florida filled with oranges bar-reled down Friendsville Street. The trucker raced through Morn-ingstar after part of I-71 was shut down because of oil spilled from a tanker. The semi killed Avery's mother, who'd been driving home from the night shift at the diner. It had been the trucker's fault, blow-ing through a stop sign. Still, now, when I drive on Friendsville, I think of those oranges rolling on the road after the accident, the force of it so hard that the back doors of the trailer opened, spilling its con-tents.

Now Avery was an especially sad story. Her father—who'd been a good boy, so smart and handsome—died over in Iraq, the first time we were there. All she had left after her mother's death was her grand-father, but he was forgetful and soon that forgetfulness turned into senility. Even at four years old, Avery could take care of him bet-ter than he could take care of her. It must be said that Avery was ex-traordinary, the smartest girl maybe to be born in Morningstar, and at four she was already reading real books with chapters. It was up to us, then, as a town, to step in, to care for Avery and her grandpa Earl. For the next twelve years, we worked on a rotating schedule, cooking Av-ery and Earl dinner, packing Avery's lunches, making sure everything was OK. Each Friday afternoon, Missy Carlton dropped off a sack of library books and picked up another sack of books that Avery had read during the week. We sewed her costumes for school plays, took her to Miss Betty's to get her hair cut, and when she was sixteen Logan Pierce taught her how to drive in his Volvo. We'd assigned him the task of driving instruction because we'd heard Volvos were the safest cars.

When Avery was ten years old, she rang the doorbell of the Ladybug one Friday after school. I opened the door and saw her, hair in two tidy braids, white button-down shirt still crisp after a day of school, Mary Janes unscuffed. I smiled. "You don't have to ring the doorbell, Avery Swenson. You're like family. You just walk in whenever you want, day or night."

She nodded but said, "It's not polite to walk into other people's houses. It's trespassing."

"Well, you don't need to worry about politeness, young lady. You're the most polite person I ever met. My Izzy could take a lesson or two from you." My daughter, Isabelle, was three years older than Avery. I'd hoped that they might become friends, but Izzy had no use for Avery; she said Avery was too much of a kiss-up, won every academic prize in school, was every teacher's pet. "Mom," Izzy once said to me, "Avery *volunteered* to go outside during lunch period every day and clap the chalk out of the erasers. She's such a nerd." And Izzy, I hate to admit, was never the teacher's pet, was sloppy and undisciplined, wore her shirts untucked and painted her fingernails blue. She constantly had headphones on and listened to music too loudly blasting out of her Walkman.

"Do you want a snack?" I asked. I ushered Avery into the front hall-way and toward the kitchen.

She shook her head. "No, thank you. Would you show me how to make a bed?"

"Make a bed?" I wondered if I'd heard wrong.

"I thought you would be the best bed-making expert in town since you have to make the beds here at the bed and breakfast every day. I can make my bed, but I can't make it *well*. I'd like to learn from you, please."

I understood then what Izzy meant about Avery being every teacher's pet. She wanted to learn to do things that no one wanted to do. What other ten-year-old girl would have made such a request? I looked out the kitchen window and across the street to the stone lions at the gate of Lake College. Beyond the lions was Armstrong Hall, with its gray turrets, its blue and gold flags flying high atop them. I imagined Avery in a few years—at twelve or thirteen—pushing through the solid wooden doors of Armstrong Hall, where the science classes at Lake were held, and asking the professors to teach her how to use microscopes, how to train lab rats, how to use Bunsen burners.

"All right, Avery," I said. "If you want to make a bed with tight corners and fluffy pillows, you've come to the right place. Follow me." I led her up the stairs, and she followed, walking daintily, barely making any noise, so different from Izzy who pounded up and down the stairs dozens of times a day in her unlaced boots. Avery was an odd little girl, but I, like everyone else in town, could not help but love her.

When Avery was sixteen, her grandfather passed. This death was slow and painful, and we were all grateful when it ended. It was his time. After that, Avery said she could take care of herself. We didn't want to agree with her, but we knew she was a responsible young lady. There was some money, life insurance from her father, a settlement from her mother's death, but we wanted her to save that money for college, so we still delivered food to her front porch and dropped it off before Avery could say no.

Avery was the valedictorian of Morningstar High and received a Presidential scholarship to Ohio State. She'd chosen that over a full scholarship to Lake College. We'd hoped she'd stay and go to Lake. She could mingle with those students who drove expensive cars with license plates from Connecticut, New York, and Massachusetts, and she could prove that Morningstar was able to produce someone who could go head-to-head with those kids from private schools in the Northeast. Now I wonder if Avery had chosen Ohio State so she could have a little breathing room for a few years, so she could get away from us and become her own person. In any case, the scholarship allowed her not to worry about tuition, and it was good that she had money tucked away. She bought herself a car. She could afford books. We were sad to see Avery go to Columbus, but we knew it was for the best.

The person who was saddest to see Avery go was Caleb Barlow. It might not be kind to say that he was slow, but that's the truth. He was the sweetest boy around, gentle, loved animals. He was in the same grade as Avery. On graduation day, Avery gave her valedictorian speech, and Caleb received an award. He was the first student in the history of Morningstar to never miss a single day of school from kindergarten all the way through twelfth grade. Everyone cheered when the principal handed him a certificate. We clapped so loudly and cheered so hard that Caleb handed his certificate back to the principal and put his hands over his ears, but it was OK because he was smiling, as overwhelmed as he was.

Everyone knew Caleb had been in love with Avery since pretty much the beginning of time. Well, everyone except Avery. Avery never seemed interested in much except her books. On some Friday nights, she and some girls from the track team would go to the movies at the single-screen theater downtown, but most Friday nights she was at home studying. She'd never had a boyfriend in Morningstar, and that was just fine. She didn't need to get herself into trouble that way, didn't need to get pregnant like those trashy girls who lived past Bowman Lane, the ones who sat on their porches eating greasy potato chips out of large bags and hooting at men driving by. Bowman was just three blocks away from Lake College; it was where the town turned from the well-kept faculty houses that surrounded the school to the run-down, dilapidated houses that the students from the college rushed by if they were headed to a movie or the ice cream shop or the bank downtown. Avery's house was only a block up from Bowman, and I was always glad she never let herself drift down the street, never got involved with the high school dropouts.

Caleb followed Avery around town, hanging around her in the library or the drugstore. Avery was always kind to Caleb, but she didn't seem to understand how much he cared for her. When she left for college, Caleb moped around town all day. A couple of weeks after she left, he found a job working for some of the Amish down the way, caring for their chickens. It was good that Caleb had found a job; his father had been out of work and depressed since the broom factory closed down, and at least Caleb was able to bring some money into the house, however little it was. The Amish must have had a sense about him, because they never hired anyone who wasn't their own. When we drove out of town, we saw him walking around on the farms, scattering feed, and we watched the chickens follow him everywhere he went like he was their mama hen. He was so gentle, the way he picked up the chicks, cradled them in his thin hands.

After a few months Caleb started a business delivering eggs for the Amish. He drove an old, bulky Cadillac that had belonged to his grandfather, and he could drive fine, although he always drove under the speed limit. We'd put in our orders, and on Wednesday afternoons he'd drive from house to house, delivering our eggs. I always made lemonade, extra sweet, when I knew he was on the way with my eggs.

Caleb was happiest during Avery's breaks from school, when she'd come back to town. She always took Caleb out to Frost King, and she'd tell him about her life at college, and he would tell her about the chickens and the egg business. He'd order a soft-serve vanilla cone, and she'd eat a bowl of strawberry ice cream, and when she was done, she'd put her chin in her palm and listen to Caleb as if his stories about baby chicks and delivering eggs were the most interesting stories she'd ever heard.

No one was happier than Caleb to hear that Avery was returning to Morningstar. For the week before Avery's return in late July, he gave everyone thirteen eggs instead of the usual dozen, cradling the extra egg carefully on top of the carton as he walked from his car to our front doors. I thought a lot about Avery and Caleb that week, thought about how we hardly knew her anymore. Four years away was a long time. Maybe she had a boyfriend. Maybe she was even engaged. What would that do to Caleb? It would be OK if these things happened far away—we could shield Caleb from them—but what would he do if she brought some boy home with her? It was a relief when Avery arrived home alone. She took Caleb out for banana splits after she found a wire basket filled with six dozen eggs on her porch the afternoon of her return.

After they'd finished at Frost King, Caleb and Avery walked to the center of town and stood outside the Brilliance Café. Caleb waved his arms and crashed his body into the glass building. He did it again and again, and finally Avery pulled him to her and held him tightly. Caleb was crying, big, heaving sobs, his face sloppy. He had been telling Avery about the birds. Just like the rest of us, the birds couldn't understand that glass building right there in the middle of Friendsville Street. They flew into the Brilliance Café since they couldn't tell the difference between glass and sky. There were often dead birds on the sidewalk. Sometimes we'd see Miller with a snow shovel, scooping those birds up. He'd slide the birds onto his shovel, carry them to the Dumpster out back, and heave them in like last week's leftovers.

A few weeks before Avery's return, Caleb drove down Friendsville Street, on his way to deliver two dozen eggs to Mrs. Crenshaw, and saw Miller with his shovel standing over a dead bird. Caleb parked his car crookedly and ran to Miller.

"What are you doing?" Caleb said.

"These birds," Miller said, waving down at three dead blackbirds, "they're a pain."

"You're killing the birds?" said Caleb.

"*I'm* not doing anything. They're too stupid to know not to fly into buildings."

Caleb bristled at the word "stupid." Everyone in Morningstar knew he didn't like it. Years ago, I spanked my own daughter for using the word about Caleb. He wasn't a quick thinker, but he wasn't stupid. He didn't have a brain that cranked fast like Avery's, but there were things he knew how to do, things he was good at.

"Are you going to bury them?" Caleb said.

Miller laughed, hard and dry. "Bury them? Yeah, sure, and I'll have a funeral, too."

"What do you do with them?" Caleb said.

"Dumpster," Miller said, pointing toward the back of the building.

"Oh," said Caleb. He took a step backward and then he began to cry, his mouth open, spit dribbling out.

"Oh, God," Miller said. "Please don't cry." I think this was when Miller finally realized something about Caleb, maybe understood he wasn't just a young punk giving him a hard time.

"Hey," Miller said, his voice softening. "It's OK."

Caleb shook his head, didn't say anything more. He sniffled hard.

"Listen, you want some pizza? Free pizza?" Miller said.

"I like Joe's pizza," Caleb said.

"You and everyone else in town." Miller sighed and put his shovel down on the sidewalk. "Look, I'll buy you a slice of Joe's pizza. Truce?"

Caleb's tears had started drying, but he was still sucking in big gasps of air. "You can't buy a slice. You have to buy a pie."

"Who doesn't sell slices? You can't walk down a block in New York without seeing some place selling slices. What if you just want one slice of pizza?"

"Then you share the rest of the pie with your family," Caleb said.

Now it was Miller's turn to shake his head. "Of course," he said. "Because everyone has a goddamn family around here." His voice was sharp again.

"I have to go," Caleb said, backing farther away, as if he were afraid Miller might hit him. "The eggs in the car are going to get hot."

He turned and headed back to the Cadillac. Miller stood on the sidewalk and watched as Caleb pulled back onto Friendsville Street. When Caleb was gone, Miller picked up his shovel, scooped up the dead blackbirds, and carried them to the Dumpster.

———

After that, I'd see Caleb slowly driving down Friendsville several times a day. If I stepped out onto the porch and craned my neck, I could see all the way downtown, could see the front of the Brilliance Café. If there were any dead birds on the sidewalk, Caleb would park, slip on a pair of thick leather gloves, and place the birds in a burlap sack.

One afternoon, Logan Pierce, the high school math teacher, followed Caleb, kept close behind Caleb's Cadillac in his red Volvo that Avery had learned to drive in six years before. Logan told me that he followed Caleb all the way to Harding Cemetery, where Caleb's mother had been buried when Caleb was fifteen. Caleb parked in a visitor's spot, and Logan watched him haul a heavy-looking sack out of the Cadillac's trunk. Caleb put his gloves on and grabbed a gardening shovel from the trunk and walked toward his mother's gravestone. Logan got out of his car and followed. He stood under a weeping willow and watched as Caleb dug up a small patch of grass near his mother's grave. Then he reached into his burlap sack and took out one of those small egg cartons, the kind for just a half dozen eggs. He opened it like a coffin and put a sparrow in. Then he gently placed the closed egg carton in the ground. Logan squinted and saw other patches of missing grass near Beverly Barlow's grave and realized it wasn't the first time Caleb had done this. He jogged up to where Caleb was digging another hole for the next grave.

"Caleb," Logan said.

"Oh, Mr. Pierce," Caleb said. "Hello." He blinked up at him.

"You can't do this," Logan said. "People put a lot of effort into keeping this grass looking nice."

"But he's putting the birds in the Dumpster."

Logan nodded and thought hard about what to do. Then he got down on his knees and helped Caleb bury the rest of the birds. When they had smoothed moist soil over the birds' graves, Logan stood, held out a hand to Caleb, and helped him up. "We'll figure something out," Logan said. "We'll figure out what to do about the birds."

Logan went to the Brilliance Café to talk to Miller the next day. He asked him to put bird silhouettes on the window, the kind that let birds understand there's something solid in front of them. He even brought some silhouettes he'd bought at Lowe's. Miller told Logan he'd spent his life savings on the Brilliance Café, paid a lot for that clear glass, spent an hour each day wiping fingerprints off it, and he wasn't going to ruin all of that with ugly bird cutouts.

"Please," Logan said. "I'm asking you as a favor."

Miller shook his head.

"You really can't?" Logan said.

Miller shook his head again and said, "I won't."

For the next few weeks, Caleb drove by and picked up the dead birds. He'd show up in the morning before Miller arrived and then return in the afternoons when Miller was pacing back and forth between the kitchen and the dining area. Miller had cut back on his staff. There was just the chef and one waitress per shift. Sometimes Miller let the chef go home early because he knew how to cook everything on the menu himself. Someone heard that he'd gone to culinary school in France for two years after he'd made all his money and quit his job on Wall Street.

The only people who still went to the Brilliance Café were from the college, and the only day the restaurant was busy was when Lu-anne Gilcrest retired from the Admissions Office and the entire office came out for a celebratory lunch. Miller brought pizza after pizza out. He smiled, and everyone noticed for the first time that despite the too-round head, he was handsome when he wasn't scowling. No one in town had ever seen Miller so happy before, so excited. Some of the women from the Admissions Office said that Miller was really a lovely young man, and his attitude problems were just a result of his money troubles and a sense of being unwelcome in Morningstar. They were convincing, but not convincing enough to get me to go to the Brilliance Café, especially in light of the bird issue.

And the bird issue was certainly still a problem. Logan Pierce knew Caleb couldn't keep digging up the soil around his mother's grave like some gopher, so he offered his backyard for Caleb's burials. Of course

Mary Pierce was furious about Caleb coming by every few days with his shovel and tearing up her flowerbeds, but what could she do? She told us that someone else had better step up once her backyard was filled. She said this loudly while standing in line at the bank, looking directly at Nancy Stables, who owned twelve acres right on the edge of town. Nancy stared down hard at the check in her hand.

So once Avery got back to town and Caleb explained everything, Avery stormed into the Brilliance Café and gave Miller an earful. Her face got red and she kept pointing at the windows and at Caleb, who waited for her on the sidewalk. It didn't take long before Miller began to nod, saying, "OK, OK, OK."

The next afternoon, Avery sat at one of those long wooden tables in the Brilliance Café with a stack of black construction paper and a pair of scissors. Every once in a while Miller walked by the table and stopped to examine Avery's work. She cut out all sorts of birds, some small, some big with wide wingspans. After a few hours, Miller and Avery stood on chairs and taped the birds all over the glass walls. They laughed as they worked. At one point, Avery reached up high, her shirt lifting to expose a line of belly, and Miller jumped off his chair and grabbed Avery's sides to make sure she didn't fall. After they finished, they shared a pizza, one of those extravagant ones, with morel mushrooms, ricotta cheese, and baby asparagus. The two of them ate it all while sharing a carafe of red wine, drinking until their cheeks got pink.

After that afternoon, things changed. Birds stopped flying into the Brilliance Café. Avery's cutouts did the trick. The more significant change, of course, was that Avery took up with Miller. Maybe we should have expected it. She'd spent four years in the city, and when she returned, we must have seemed awfully quiet and dull to her compared to Miller with his glass building and exotic ingredients. I could show her how to fold a fitted sheet, Missy Carlton could teach her the Dewey Decimal System, Logan Pierce could explain the Pythagorean theorem. But how could we ever compare to Miller?

Before the school year started, we'd see Avery sitting in the Brilliance Café drinking iced tea and working on lesson plans. Sometimes Miller would stand behind her, massaging her shoulders, leaning down to kiss the top of her head before he went back to the kitchen. In the evenings, after the few customers left, they would dance slowly in the darkened restaurant lit only by a few flickering candles on the tabletops, spinning around and around. Why would Avery so boldly display herself in the glass restaurant? What bothered us most was that Caleb could see all of it. Some nights he walked by outside the Brilliance Café with his gloves and burlap sack, but there were no birds anymore. There was nothing for him to do but walk slowly and watch Avery and Miller and all that love right on display.

We were sure Caleb's car accident in September was because of his devastation. He crashed the Cadillac on Pine Street, smashed right into a telephone pole. If we hadn't known Caleb, we would have thought he was drunk, but everyone knew Caleb didn't drink. The car was too twisted to be salvaged. Caleb, unsurprisingly, was perfectly fine. As a child, he tripped on uneven sidewalks, toppled off his bike, fell off ladders, and there was never a sprain or broken bone. At worst he'd have a few scratches. "That's my miracle boy," his father would say after every one of Caleb's accidents. Even though Caleb was fine, his car was totaled, and this was a problem because Caleb had been doing well with his egg deliveries. We all wanted to help, but what could we do? There were no jobs to spare in Morningstar.

Avery persuaded Miller to hire Caleb as a busboy. She told him it would just be until Caleb made enough money to buy a used car and could get back to delivering eggs. She must have told Miller that it would be impossible for the Barlows to survive with both Caleb and his father out of work. So Miller hired Caleb, and it became his job to spray the windows every morning and make sure there were no fingerprints. He also had to load the dishwasher, wipe down the tables, and sweep the floor. We saw him sweeping slowly and carefully, and we could just see the hurt drip off of him when Avery and Miller were there together.

It went on this way for over a month, until right before Halloween. The Brilliance Café was doing better business because the college kids were back. Miller bought an espresso machine and started serving expensive coffee drinks, and the college kids hauled their laptops to the café and spent hours sipping coffee and typing away. Miller developed a good relationship with the people at the college, and they used him to cater their events, and he seemed to get happier as he got busier. Avery seemed happy too, spending the late afternoons grading papers and drinking espresso at the table right by the front of the restaurant.

Before they headed to Miller's house each evening, Avery and Miller would still slowly dance in the restaurant. We could hear the music they liked to play when we walked by on the street; it was something bluesy, with a syrup-voiced female singer who sounded mournful. It was strange music for young people to like. Sometimes we'd see them sway in one spot and kiss. We still didn't understand how Avery could be so thoughtless, especially since most nights while they danced Caleb was in the kitchen loading the dishwasher. But then, suddenly, the dancing stopped. I thought it was because of a conversation Miller and Avery had at the diner one night while they were eating pumpkin pie.

Miller had a strange way of eating his pie. First he took the crimped edge of the crust off and ate that like it was a breadstick. Then he used his fork to turn the pie upside down and scraped off the rest of the crust and ate that, leaving a quivering hunk of pumpkin on his plate, which he ate with a spoon. Avery laughed, and Miller shrugged and said, "I was raised by wolves."

"I didn't know there were wolves in Brooklyn," Avery said.

Evelyn Anderson came to refill their coffee mugs and said, "Caleb came by for supper earlier. I've never seen that boy look sadder." Evelyn had been Avery's mother's friend, worked side by side with her at the diner for five years before her death, and she didn't like the idea of Avery and Miller together. She thought he was trouble and would complain about him to anyone who'd listen.

"He must be sad about his car," said Avery. "It belonged to his grandpa, you know."

"Oh, honey, that's not what he's sad about." Evelyn raised her eyebrows dramatically at Avery and pointed one sharp red fingernail at Avery, then at Miller.

"Can I have another slice of pie?" Miller said.

Evelyn paused for a moment.

"Please?" he said. He flashed her his too-white, too-straight smile.

"Anything you want," Evelyn said coldly, and headed back to the counter. "You get anything you want."

Avery waited a second, then said, "What was that about?"

"I'm still hungry."

"I mean the Caleb stuff. Why is she mad at you?"

Miller sighed. "You don't know?"

"Know what?" Avery said.

"I thought you were the smartest girl in town."

Avery shook her head. "Come on. Tell me what you're getting at."

Evelyn slid another slice of pie in front of Miller, then went back through the swinging door into the kitchen.

"Caleb is in love with you. And everyone is upset with me for stealing you from him."

Avery laughed, clear and high, innocent. "That's just silly." And here was the thing about Avery: she was the smartest girl in town, got the best grades, whipped through book after book, but sometimes she wasn't smart about the everyday things. Like how she hadn't known volunteering to clean the erasers instead of running around on the playground during recess would make the other children resent her.

"It's not silly to Caleb," Miller said. "You see the way he looks at you?"

"He's like a brother. I've known him forever."

"Then he's probably been in love with you forever."

Avery sat silently while Miller chewed on his pie crust, and finally she said softly, "How could I never have known?"

Miller's fourth mistake was hosting the Halloween party. Every Halloween, the Student Activities Committee at Lake College threw a big party. Usually they held it in the basement of the student center, but it had flooded earlier in the fall, so they rented the Brilliance Café for the night. The students would pay for the space, and they'd put in an order for two hundred pizzas. Miller hired people from Cleveland to help cook and serve. He knew enough not to try to hire anyone from Morningstar.

Each year the Halloween party had a ridiculous theme—Space Robots, Buried Underwater Ship, Japanese Disco—and the students raised money for an entire year to pay for the DJ and decorations. The party in the Brilliance Café was themed Haunted Forest. They were going to clear out the tables and bring in fake trees, the kind they have in the rides in Disneyland so the indoors could look just like the outdoors. They would spread twinkling white lights across the ceiling to look like stars, and everyone would dance under the fake starlight.

For a week before the party, trucks kept arriving with more parts of the forest. First they laid out a thick brown carpet to look like the forest floor. Then the trees came: pine, ash, maple, elm. They were so lifelike that if you didn't get up close and examine them, you'd swear they were real. The day before the party, a white van pulled up outside the restaurant, and two men brought in a dozen owls.

"Awesome!" said one of the Lake students who was helping to set up. "They look totally real!"

A squat man chewing on the end of a drinking straw while carrying one of the owls said, "They *are* real, boy. You understand what taxidermy is?"

"I meant they looked alive." The student reached out a finger to touch the owl's wing, and the man turned in a half circle and shielded the bird.

"Best not to touch it. You're just renting these," the man said.

The two men climbed ladders and settled the owls high up in the trees. Those birds were the perfect touch, all of them staring down with their round yellow eyes watching everything beneath them, making the forest actually look a little haunted.

Miller's Duskman's fifth mistake was taking down those bird silhouettes Avery had made. Miller and Caleb climbed on chairs and peeled the tape off the birds, and then Caleb scrubbed the glass, trying to remove the stickiness left behind. While he was cleaning the glass, one of the owls caught his eye and then another and then another. He waited until Miller disappeared into the kitchen, then brought a ladder to one of the pine trees. He climbed the ladder and softly touched an owl. It was the calmest looking one, its wings tucked into its body, its head slightly tilted. Caleb ran his hands over and over that bird until Miller came back out of the kitchen, holding a can of solvent. I thought he'd yell at Caleb for touching the rented owl, but he just held the ladder steady while Caleb climbed down, and I thought maybe Miller was changing, learning how to be a decent man. After Caleb was back on the ground, Miller showed him how to put the solvent on a rag and rub the spots where the tape had been. The two of them worked together until the glass shone.

On Halloween the weather was perfectly clear. Miller and Caleb had done such a good job of polishing those windows that it hardly looked like there was any glass there; the forest seemed to have sprung up right in the middle of the sidewalk. A few hours before the party was to start, we saw Caleb crouched outside the café holding his burlap sack. The birds were back. And the trees inside, which looked so real, must have been confusing for the birds. They glided right into the window, thinking that within a few feet they'd land on a high branch. That October was especially cold, and the hawks were already in Morningstar, those magnificent birds that liked to sit high on the branches of the bare trees at Lake College. Maybe they thought they'd stumbled upon such good luck to suddenly find a forest full of lush trees. Or perhaps the hawks saw all those owls, perched comfortably on trees they thought were rightly theirs, and they wanted to claim their territory. By late afternoon Caleb had already collected four dead hawks.

Avery came to the café after she'd finished at school. She was dressed as Dorothy from *The Wizard of Oz*. When she arrived, she saw Caleb crouched on the sidewalk with his sack. He stared at her. She looked beautiful with her dark hair in two braids, the blue dress, the sparkling red shoes. Ever since Miller had told Avery that Caleb loved her, she'd acted strange around Caleb, like she no longer knew how to talk to him.

"More birds," Caleb said. He lifted the sack.

"I'm sorry. I'll make more cutouts after the party and I'll have Miller tape them up."

"I could help you," Caleb said.

"Oh, I don't want you to have to stay too late," said Avery. She moved her feet nervously, and she looked just like Dorothy clicking her heels together and hoping to get out of Oz. "You've been working so hard."

"It's OK," Caleb said. "I can help."

"We'll see. Maybe you'll be tired by then."

Caleb said nothing and followed Avery inside, clutching the full burlap sack.

By eight o'clock, the waiters and cooks Miller hired had arrived. Everyone wore brown from head to toe, maybe to make them blend right into the forest. The party wouldn't start until ten, but there was still a lot of work to do. There were balls of pizza dough lined up on racks behind Miller. The pizzas would be made fresh: tossed, topped, and slid into that Italian oven right before being served.

Caleb's job was to collect tickets, which had been sold on campus. All Caleb had to do was stand by the door, take the tickets, and drop them into a basket. At nine thirty he took his post. He held his empty wicker basket, waiting for the first students to arrive. He looked down the street toward the college for a minute, but then his head turned and he stared inside the restaurant. At first it seemed he was looking at Avery; she was mixing a large bowl of Sprite, fruit punch, and rainbow sherbet. But then we noticed the tilt of his neck and understood that he was looking up at those owls up in the trees. He was fascinated by those birds, which seemed frozen halfway between alive and dead.

It was calm for a few minutes, exceptionally quiet, and Avery mixed and mixed the sherbet into the punch bowl, the waiters dried glasses and stacked small plates on the counter, and Caleb stared at the birds. And then Miller crashed through the side door, holding Caleb's burlap sack high in the air. It swung back and forth from the weight of the hawks. Miller got close to Caleb's face and shouted, "What is this?"

"Birds," Caleb said. He tried to take a step back, but there was nowhere to go. He was pressed up against the closed door of the Brilliance Café.

"*Dead* birds!" Miller screamed. The vein on the side of his neck bulged. He grabbed Caleb's shoulders and pushed him hard against the glass door. The bag of birds was still in Miller's hand, and it sagged heavily on Caleb's chest. "I told you to put them in the Dumpster."

"I was going to do that with them," he said, pointing up at the owls inside.

"You were going to learn taxidermy?" Miller said. He pulled Caleb away from the door by his shirt collar, dragged him onto the sidewalk, and then pushed him again, hard, into the glass on the front of the building. "Why do you have to be so stupid about everything?"

The waiters watched what was happening from inside, and Avery dropped her mixing spoon into the bowl of punch and ran outside.

"Miller!" she said. "Stop!"

"Stay out of it," Miller said. Spit flew from his mouth as he spoke. Caleb clutched the handle of his basket. He was shaking.

"Stop it, Miller Duskman," Avery said, grabbing his arm. She spoke to him in the same tone she used when her third graders were cruel to each other.

"You don't understand," he hissed, shrugging her hand off of his arm.

"Please give me the birds," Caleb said.

Miller took the bag and swung it over his head and flung it down the street. It landed with a dull thump. He returned his hands to Caleb's shoulders, pushing him into the glass.

"Do you know what this retard did?" Miller shouted.

"Stop it!" Avery said. "Don't ever say that."

"Please, let me get the birds," Caleb said. He stretched his neck so he could see the sack.

"This idiot," Miller said, "put the filthy dead birds he scraped off the sidewalk in the walk-in cooler. They were sitting on a rack between the asparagus and the eggplants, those nasty dead birds just laid out on the rack like loaves of bread. Do you understand what kind of health code violation that is? I have to throw it all away, the cheese and the tomatoes and the rest of the produce. That's thousands of dollars of food in the garbage! We have nothing now to make pizzas with. We have dough."

"It's OK," Avery said. "We'll figure something out." She looked around her. Some of the students from the college were arriving in their costumes, standing back, worried.

Miller laughed in a mean way. "There's nothing to figure out." He dragged Caleb onto the sidewalk. Caleb let his body go slack, fell to the ground. "You ruined everything."

"Stop it," Avery said again.

"You don't understand, Avery," Miller shouted. "I have nothing. I'm broke. This party was supposed to save my restaurant." He pointed to the students. "You think these kids who sit around for hours and pay for one cup of coffee are keeping this place afloat?" Miller pulled Caleb to his feet and pushed him hard into the front of the Brilliance Café. "You've ruined everything," he screamed into Caleb's face as he pulled him forward by the shoulders and then slammed him back once more into the glass.

Everyone heard the cracking. Everyone, even Nancy Stables, all the way on the edge of town. There was one large crack when Caleb's head crashed into the wall, but then the cracking kept going and going, like the ice on a frozen lake fracturing from too much weight on it. The waiters ran outside, and everyone watched as the cracks spread and spread, from one wall to the next, and for a moment, everything glowed from those twinkling lights inside, the whole thing a map of glowing cracks and crackles. Then Avery swept down and pulled Caleb to his feet and there, right in front of Miller and everyone else, she pressed her lips to Caleb's and remained unmoving for a long time, as if this one kiss could right everything that had gone wrong, as if this kiss was her apology for everything that she could not give him, and everyone watched as Miller opened his mouth to say something but nothing came out. Then the cracking stopped and it was absolutely silent for one second and then the glass walls fell on all sides of the Brilliance Café, and shards of glass blanketed the whole forest, over all those trees and owls, glass plunged into the punch bowl, into the empty cups, and covered the brown carpet that lined the forest floor.

Miller Duskman's final mistake was not fighting for Avery. Afterwards, after the Halloween dance had been cancelled and the Brilliance Café had crumbled and all the waiters had been sent home, Miller wept, told Avery, "This town has changed me. I'm not like this."

Avery shook her head, walked away.

"Don't go, please," Miller said, but Avery continued to walk down the block, her sparkling red shoes glowing in the moonlight. The sound of her footsteps echoed down the street.

I think Avery could have come to forgive Miller if he'd just chased after her that night, had followed her down the street and begged her to understand his side of the story. He could have told her how we ignored him when we passed him on the sidewalk, how we'd boycotted his café. I understand now that the party had meant something to him; he'd prepared for it for a long time, and he'd thought it might change his relationship with the town. But he didn't chase after her. Miller stayed on the sidewalk the entire night, cried until he fell asleep, right there next to the forest that had been rained upon by slivers of glass.

Miller was lucky Caleb had that miracle body. Logan Pierce helped Caleb into his Volvo and took him to the hospital after the Brilliance Café crumbled, and the doctors said everything was fine with Caleb, inside and out. Some people told Caleb he should sue Miller for assault, but Caleb said he wanted to forget about it all.

When the men from the taxidermy shop came to pick up their owls, Logan talked to them, told them Caleb was a good worker and loved animals, wasn't afraid to touch dead ones, and asked if they might let him do an internship with them. "An internship?" said the squat one. "What do you think we are, the White House?" But then he agreed after Logan told him the whole story about the birds and the egg carton coffins and the burlap sack and the cracked glass. "We could use an extra pair of hands, but we can't pay him much," the man said. It was OK, though; Caleb didn't need money to buy a car anymore. Miller had given Caleb his car, had taken care of the paperwork so it could belong to Caleb, and left it parked in the Barlows' driveway and put the key in the mailbox.

So now Caleb had a car and could deliver eggs on Wednesdays and could drive the thirty miles out of town to learn taxidermy on the other days. It was good, we thought, for him to spend as little time in Morningstar as possible. He didn't need to be around Avery. There was something about that kiss that changed everything. Everyone knew that it didn't mean that Caleb and Avery could be together, but it had altered the balance of things.

Two days after the Brilliance Café crumbled, Miller was gone. He'd rented a U-Haul, packed all night, and left. Everyone thought he'd gone back to New York. We all knew he wasn't coming back. He'd loved Avery—we understood that—and Avery had loved him, and if they'd been in another place maybe things would have worked out differently.

Once she'd sold her house to a young political science professor at the college, Avery was gone, too. We realized later that the kiss was really a long, wordless goodbye to the only person that Avery would miss when she left Morningstar. Eileen Cord, who was the long-term substitute the school district called whenever one of the teachers went on maternity leave, took over Avery's class. A week after Avery left, a construction crew ripped up the remnants of the Brilliance Café, and then there was just an empty spot where it had once stood.

Right after Avery left, I sent her an e-mail telling her that she'd always have a room at the Ladybug Bed and Breakfast if she wanted to come back to town. "Stay as long as you like. I know you know how to make beds ☺" I wrote. I waited months and months and got no reply. A postcard with an image of a yak on the front and foreign stamps on the back finally came the next fall, and Avery asked me to pass it around to everyone who'd cared for her when she was a little girl. She'd joined the Peace Corps and was in Mongolia, as far away as she could go. She said she hadn't spoken to Miller since he'd left Morningstar; she'd added that part, I knew, because she understood that we'd want to know whether she and Miller had met up somewhere, continued their romance. "Thank you all for caring for me for so many years," she wrote, "but please know that I just can't come back anymore."

I manned the apple dumpling stand at the Harvest Festival that October and passed the postcard around to the people who'd gathered around me. It moved from hand to hand, each person reading quickly and passing the postcard on. No one said anything; it was hard to figure out the right words. We knew we hadn't been hospitable to Miller. He'd seen something in the town, had liked the place enough to open his restaurant here, and we should have been kinder. If we'd treated Miller better, that awfulness never would have happened with Caleb, and we wouldn't have lost Avery.

I looked at the postcard when it returned to my hands, stared at the yak and was reminded of Miller's buffalo milk mozzarella. Then I thought about that Halloween party and Avery's sparkling red shoes walking right out of town. And then I knew we were the ones who'd made the worst mistakes of all.

Half and Half Club

It was Sparrow Sanderson who ruined Mrs. Cook's first planned activity for the Half and Half Multicultural Club. Mrs. Cook wanted to ask the club members to bring in photographs of themselves and separate photographs of each of their parents. She would pin photos of the parents in random order above photos of the students on the bulletin board in the history hallway. Then she'd put cutout letters over the photographs spelling WHO ARE MY PARENTS? People would have to figure out that Priti and Priya Fitzgerald belonged to the mother in a bright pink sari and the green-eyed, freckled Irish father. Or they could deduce that Lily Stern went with the Chinese woman with the stick-straight black hair and Dr. David Stern, smiling out from the photograph Mrs. Cook always saw in the local Sunday paper advertising Stern Podiatric Clinic. But Sparrow had thwarted her plan by showing up for the club's second meeting last week. Sparrow Sanderson, vaguely Asian looking, vaguely Mexican looking, was the adopted son of Florence and Homer Sanderson. If she put Sparrow's photograph up, WHO ARE MY PARENTS? would be a cruel question that could not be answered. Mrs. Cook stared at the bulletin board. So what, now, should she do with this empty space?

Mrs. Cook hadn't wanted to be the faculty advisor for the Half and Half Multicultural Club, but the principal, Dr. Hargrave, had reminded her that her responsibilities at Sun Meadow High School included participation in the extracurricular life of the school. Mrs.

Cook had been at the school for four years teaching tenth and eleventh grade history and, because of her lack of experience in athletics or yearbooking or newspapering, had not been asked to coach or supervise anything. But then Dr. Hargrave had called her into his office in September and told her he had a wonderful opportunity for her. "You know I'm white, right?" Mrs. Cook said. "Like a hundred percent white?"

Dr. Hargrave stared at her for too long without speaking then said, "As one of our star history and social studies teachers, I thought you might have some interest in other cultures." And what could she say to that? Of course she had to agree.

On his way back from the men's lavatory, Dr. Hargrave spotted Beatrice Cook standing by an empty bulletin board with a blank expression on her face. He could forgive her for this. When his wife was pregnant, she'd been forgetful, walking into a room for something and then unable to recall what she'd wanted.

Beatrice raised a hand to steady herself against the wall, and Dr. Hargrave wondered if it was advisable for Beatrice to be the only chaperone at the Half and Half Club's community service trip to the nursing home that coming weekend. How far along was she? Dr. Hargrave should know; the job ad for a long-term substitute for Beatrice's classes had been sitting on his desk for weeks. He'd need to attend to this soon. She looked at least eight months pregnant.

Beatrice was pale, had red hair and a long, thin nose. She reminded him of the FBI agent on that X-Files show his daughter liked to watch on Friday nights. When the outside assessors had told Dr. Hargrave that Sun Meadow High School should pay more attention to multiculturalism—after all, they were halfway through the 1990s, not in the Dark Ages—he'd decided that despite Beatrice's glowing whiteness, she should helm the Half and Half Club since she was not involved in any other school activities. It would have been ideal, of course, for there to be a mixed-race teacher who could advise the club, but there was no one on the faculty that fit the bill.

Down the hall came Danny Cooper, math teacher and football coach, dragging a mesh sack bulging with footballs. He was round-faced and heavy with a foot-dragging walk, and it was nearly impossible to believe that less than a decade ago he'd been the quarterback at Sun Meadow High. He'd been a superstar, the golden boy, handsome and charming, with an arm like a cannon. Rumors swirled about how he'd seduced each of the prettiest girls in the high school and then ditched them, one after another. Now he was only twenty-five, but the poor boy was already nearly bald, only a fuzzy sprinkling of blond hairs left on his pink scalp. How the mighty had fallen. He was a good coach, knew his football, even though his own career had fizzled at Kansas State. He'd been such an amazing athlete in high school, so full of potential, and it had been no surprise that he'd gotten a football scholarship. People in Sun Meadow, Kansas, were sure the NFL was in Danny Cooper's future. Dr. Hargrave had heard that a girl in college had broken Danny's heart, and he had never been able to recover. He'd fallen into a deep depression, hadn't been able to pull himself back together either physically or mentally. But now he'd been able to coach his team to three straight sectional championships, which provided great newspaper coverage for the school. Danny was good for the school's reputation, but Dr. Hargrave wished math wasn't such a problem for him. Danny taught the ninth grade math classes and had somehow managed to graduate from college with a math degree, but now he had trouble with numbers. The school district was paying for Danny to take classes at Sun Meadow Community College. The money came from the Professional Development Fund, and Dr. Hargrave was glad that so far none of the nosey secretaries had asked what sort of professional development Danny was pursuing.

"Danny," Dr. Hargrave said, clamping a hand on Danny's shoulder. "A word?"

"Sure," Danny said, and Dr. Hargrave led him into his office. Danny set the bag of footballs against a wall and slumped into the seat across from Dr. Hargrave.

"Beatrice Cook is taking the Half and Half Club to the Sun Meadow Senior Home on Sunday, and I hoped you'd be willing to co-chaperone. About a dozen students are going, and it might be too many kids for one person to handle. And in light of her advanced pregnancy, it would be wonderful to have someone strong and capable to assist."

Danny's eyes were focused on the blotter on Dr. Hargrave's desk. "Can't you go with her?"

Dr. Hargrave shook his head vigorously. "My daughter has a ballet recital." This wasn't true. His daughter was thirteen and sullen. On Sunday, she'd probably spend the afternoon painting her fingernails black and ringing her eyes with eyeliner until she looked like a raccoon. She might also take the opportunity to dye her hair another bright and unattractive color, leaving a stain of pink or purple dye in the bathroom sink. Dr. Hargrave's wife had passed away three years before, and now he was often at a loss about how to raise his daughter alone. In the last year, she'd turned into a strange, unknowable creature. He dreaded next year, when she'd be in the high school, *his* high school.

Danny squirmed in his seat, reminding Dr. Hargrave of the troubled boys who were sent to his office for fighting. "Isn't there anyone else who could do it?" Danny said.

Dr. Hargrave fixed Danny with his serious stare, the one he used on teenage delinquents. In the beginning, after he'd taken this position twenty-five years ago, he'd spent time each night practicing the stare in the bathroom mirror. His wife had understood exactly what he was doing when she caught him glaring at his own reflection. She'd found it hilarious. But back then he'd been goofy and idealistic, and the stare didn't fit his face the way it did now. Now his job mostly consisted of routine discipline, endless meetings, and too much paperwork. His face had become lined, and he had bags under his eyes; he now possessed a perfect countenance from which to project disapproving stares. When he'd begun as principal of Sun Meadow High School, he thought he could inspire kids, help them improve their lives. Now he was no longer so idealistic, so foolish as to think he could change the world. Dr. Hargrave counted to seven silently, then said, "How are the math classes going at the community college? Enlightening?"

"Fine," Danny said. "Fine. I'll chaperone."

Something unusual happened on Friday: Priti and Priya Fitzgerald walked home from school together. On days when Priti could get a ride from some boy, she'd just leave, not even let Priya know where she was going and who she was going with. Priya would wait outside the high school for fifteen, twenty minutes, and when she'd decided that Priti wasn't showing up, she'd head off alone. Priya knew that the boys called her sister Pretty Priti. These same boys ignored Priya. But how could Priti be considered pretty and Priya be considered nothing? They had the same face. They were both exactly five feet four inches tall and weighed one hundred nineteen pounds. They were identical twins, formed almost eighteen years ago from the same zygote. But there was something about Priti that drew the boys in and something about Priya that told the boys to stay away.

On most days, when Priya got home and their mother asked where her sister was, Priya shrugged and said, "Some school thing, I think." Then she'd go to her room and work on her college admissions essays and tell herself that if she worked hard enough she could escape to a good college far away. She wanted, so badly, to leave Sun Meadow. She was tired of lying to her parents for Priti, tired of how unchallenging her classes were at school, tired of the girls in her grade who only wanted to get married and have babies, as if there was nothing better to do in life. Things would be better somewhere else.

"Gross," Priti said, pointing down. There was a dead rabbit, bloody and mauled, on the sidewalk. This was the third one they'd seen on the walk home.

"Gross?" said Priya. "How about tragic?"

The dead rabbits were Priti's fault. The Sandersons' German shepherd had been howling after dark for weeks, and two nights ago Priti had snuck into Priya's room and shaken her awake. "You want to help me do something about this?" Priti said.

Priya had blinked at the silhouette of her twin sister outlined by the bright moonlight. She thought of when they were small, when they'd shared a room. Back then, their father had joked that they'd shared a brain, too. As toddlers, they'd had a language that was all their own, and they'd babble constantly, cracking each other up. Their father said, "It was worse than when your mother is with her sisters, all of them speaking Hindi. At least I'd have some chance of learning that language. With you two and your secret language, I had no hope." Now, though, their secret language had been long forgotten.

"What are you going to do?" Priya said, pushing herself up in bed. She wondered if her sister was high or drunk. She knew that when Priti went off with boys, she smoked weed and drank vodka. Maybe she planned to get the dog high.

"Don't look at me all wide-eyed. I'm not going to *kill* the dog."

"What do you want me to do?" Priya said.

"Come with me."

"It's three a.m." And yet it was a tempting offer. When was the last time her sister had asked her to do something together?

"Exactly. We have to get up for school in three and a half hours. And if this stupid dog keeps me up for another night, I'm going to pass out in Physics."

"Is Sparrow going to be there?" Priya asked. Priya—although she would not admit it, especially to Priti—harbored a secret crush on Sparrow Sanderson, who seemed too delicate to possibly exist in the same universe as the loud, lunky boys who charged down the hallways of Sun Meadow High. She felt a kinship to him, believed they both belonged far away from Sun Meadow, in a place where people appreciated quiet, contemplative thinkers.

"I'm sure Sparrow is going to be snug in his bed. His nest. Whatever it is that sparrows sleep in. Are you coming or not?"

"What are you going to do?"

"I'm letting the dog out of their yard. That dog needs to run free," Priti said.

Priti was dressed completely in black, like some cat burglar. She pulled the hood of her sweatshirt over her head. "You coming or not?"

"I think you should go back to sleep. Put some ear plugs in." The last thing Priya needed was to get caught committing a crime. If that happened, she would have a criminal record, and then she'd never get into a good college.

"Why are you so lame?" Priti said. She pulled the strings tight on her hood so only her dark eyes, her nose, and her pursed lips peeked out.

"I'm just tired," said Priya. Then she watched her sister slip out the bedroom window, reaching for a thick branch on the tree outside, sneaking out as if she were one of those mischievous teenagers in the movies Priya liked to watch with her mother on Friday nights when Priti was out doing who knows what.

It was bad enough that they were stuck walking home from school together—usually Priti got a ride from some boy or another—but now Priya was in lecture mode, and Priti wished her sister would shut up about the rabbits. Yes, there was a correlation. Yes, she'd let the Sandersons' German shepherd out two nights ago and there were dead rabbits up and down the street and the dog was sort of missing but not really because it was obviously chewing up the local rabbit population in the middle of the night. And maybe for uptight Priya this was a tragedy, but at least the dog was taking out its aggression on rabbits instead of howling at the moon.

"What, you're an animal rights activist?" Priti said. "Or are you, like, a vegetarian now? Like our aunties?" She wanted a cigarette but knew that if she even reached for the carton in her backpack she'd get lectured by Priya about the dangers of smoking.

"No, I'm not a vegetarian. I'm just saying that these dead rabbits seem . . . unnecessary."

"That stupid dog's barking was unnecessary. Do you know that he was supposed to be a police dog but he was too retarded and got kicked out of police dog training? The Sandersons took him in because they can't help but adopt retarded things," Priti said. She knew she was being cruel. Her sister had an obvious crush on Sparrow Sanderson. This crush was befuddling, since Sparrow almost never talked, and when he did, he stuttered. And he was named after a bird, the lamest bird of all. If you had to be named after a bird, it should be something like Hawk or Eagle.

Priti watched Priya process what she'd just said. She waited to see if Priya would argue or try to stand up for Sparrow, but she remained silent. Priya bent down and picked up the rabbit's carcass with just the thumb and forefinger of each hand and moved it onto the grass.

Priti said, "Now you probably have rabbit AIDS."

"There's no such thing as rabbit AIDS."

"There's cat AIDS."

"It's called Feline Immunodeficiency Virus, and you can't transmit it from cat to human. Stop being stupid. Please. I just wanted to try to do right by the rabbit," Priya said.

Priti laughed. Do right by the rabbit. Where did her sister get these ideas? She lit a cigarette and inhaled deeply. Priya shook her head and said, "That's not good for you." The nicotine hit Priti quickly and felt good; it helped her deal with her sister's chronic annoyingness. She puffed smoke in Priya's direction, and Priya waved her arms and hacked, as if a garbage truck had spewed exhaust in her face.

"Are you going to the meeting tomorrow night?" Priya asked as they rounded the corner toward their house.

"Half Breed Club? It's so stupid, you know. Everyone's just doing it to pad up their college applications." Priti ground out her cigarette and jumped up and down, trying to get the smell of smoke off her clothes. Her mother would kill her if she knew she smoked.

"It wouldn't hurt you to have some extracurriculars," Priya said.

"I'm not going to college." She wasn't sure if this was true, but she was turned off by her sister's desperation about getting into a good college. It was all she could talk about.

Priya said, "It's an important meeting. We're planning for our Things Inside of Other Things event at the nursing home."

Priti stopped jumping and stared at her sister. "Things Inside of Other Things? What sort of perverted event is that?"

Priya sighed. "I don't like the idea of 'things' being the only noun in the title of our event, but we couldn't think of any other all-encompassing words. It's a food event. We're in charge of samosas. Rigoberto is in charge of empanadas. Lily's making dumplings. At the last meeting we were talking about the commonalities between cultures, and we noticed that most cultures had some food item that was wrapped in a crust or dough. So we'll make these things and then bring them to the nursing home to share with the senior citizens."

"What's Mrs. Cook contributing? What's a white-person thing inside another thing? A Hot Pocket?"

"Maybe you should come tomorrow night and see," Priya said.

Here was Priti, marching down the sidewalk in front of the high school in ripped fishnet stockings and a too-short jean skirt, as if she were the star of some ridiculous music video from the eighties. She puffed away on a cigarette. Lily Stern hated Priti Fitzgerald. Just a few years ago, Lily and Priti and Priya had been best friends, but now Priti was different. She was, for lack of a better word, *bad*. She did drugs and drank and, if the rumors were to be believed, slutted it up with a different boy each week. Now that their trio had fallen apart, Priti did nothing to hide the fact that she thought Priya and Lily were enormous dorks for caring about GPAs and extracurriculars and colleges. When they'd all been friends, they'd complained about their overly strict Asian mothers, who were not like the rest of the easygoing Midwestern mothers in Sun Meadow. "Can you believe it?" Priti had once said. "White people *like* hanging out with their families." It had seemed incomprehensible to all three of them. In their families, their mothers were always nagging them to get better grades, to practice their musical instruments, to write thank-you notes immediately after receiving gifts. Lily's mother even made her go to Chinese School almost an hour away in Overland Park on Saturday mornings, where she had to endlessly copy and recopy Chinese characters, as if this were a skill that would somehow help her in life. Lily and Priti and Priya had come up with a theory that if their fathers had married white women, they'd now be very different men, jovial and lenient with their children, the type who owned lake houses where they could play Battleship and UNO with their families all weekend long. They wouldn't come home from work tired and grumpy and shout, "Would you just listen to your mother!" every time there was tension in the house. They would be the type of men who'd hand out bundles of money to their children and call it "allowance." When Lily was a little girl and had asked her mother why she didn't get an allowance like her classmates, her mother had said, "We allow you to live here. We allow you to eat our food. We allow you to have a comfortable bed. We allow you to take piano lessons. You need no other allowance."

Lily waved cigarette smoke out of her face. Priti sighed, dropped her cigarette to the ground, and stomped on it with her Doc Martens boot. "So whose car are we taking?" she said.

"I can drive you," said Wendell Jackson. He'd snuck up behind Lily; she hadn't even heard him. Why was he coming to this meeting? He hadn't been to the first two meetings this fall, then he suddenly showed up ready to go to Mrs. Cook's house to spend all night making food?

"Awesome," said Priti. "A ride would be awesome."

"What are you making, Wendell?" Lily said.

He reached into the back pocket of his jeans and pulled out a piece of paper with writing on it. "Pierogies. I'm half Polish. This is my grandma's recipe. I've got a huge sack of potatoes in the car. Like fifty pounds of them."

"I didn't know you were half Polish," Lily said. During the very first meeting of the Half and Half Club, Mrs. Cook had made them go around and say what they each were. If Wendell had actually shown up, he could have shared that he was half black and half Polish. That would have been much more interesting to know than what Mrs. Cook had very seriously shared about how she was half British and half from Missouri.

Wendell shrugged. "Nobody knows much about me."

"I'd like to learn," said Priti in an obviously whorish way. But she got away with saying stuff like that all the time. Guys seemed to like it.

"You two want a ride, too?" Wendell said.

"I've got my mom's station wagon," said Lily. "I was just waiting here for Priya and Priti and anyone else who might need a ride."

Priti pulled Wendell's arm and led him to his rusty Corolla, which he'd parked in one of the teachers' spots nearest the school. They drove away together, and Lily noted that they went in the opposite direction from Mrs. Cook's house. She wondered if Wendell and Priti would even make it to the Things Inside of Other Things cooking party. "I don't know how you deal with her," she said.

"She can be all right," Priya said. "We walked home from school together yesterday. Then we walked here together tonight."

Lily hated the way Priya always defended her sister. Lily felt abandoned by Priti. She couldn't imagine how Priya really felt. It was one thing to have a friend act like she was far too cool to hang out with you; it would be another thing altogether if it was your sister. Lily's little sister, Christina, who'd been born when Lily was four, had Down Syndrome. Lily loved Christina fiercely, but even when Lily was a little girl, she'd known that she and her sister would never have that tight bond Priti and Priya had, never have their synchronicity, and this made her jealous and sad. And now Priti wanted to throw her relationship with Priya out the window. It wasn't fair.

"There's Sparrow," Priya said, pointing to the circle in front of the school where the school buses parked. Sparrow was on his skateboard. Priya waved at him, and Sparrow skated over to where they stood.

"You going to Mrs. Cook's?" Lily asked. Sparrow was part of the club, even though he might not actually be half something and half something else. But he had dark skin and had been born in Brazil and now lived with the Sandersons, who were super white, so he sort of kind of counted for the club. Sparrow nodded. "You want a ride?" Lily said. "You can come with us." Sparrow nodded again, tapped the toe of his sneaker on the edge of his skateboard, and made it fly up in the air. He grabbed it and tucked it under his arm.

"Th-th-thanks," he said. He never talked much, and Lily assumed it was because of his stutter. But usually, once he got talking, the stutter mostly went away.

They walked to the car, and Lily unlocked the doors. "I've got all the ingredients for dumplings and wontons in the front seat. It's kind of a lot of stuff. It'd probably be easier for you guys to just sit in the back instead of moving everything," she said. It really wouldn't be so hard to move the ingredients, but she knew that Priya—even though she denied it—was basically in love with Sparrow. Probably nothing would ever happen between them, because Sparrow barely talked and Priya was too shy and too determined to be the complete opposite of her slutty sister, but Lily thought it would be nice for them to sit next to each other, even if just for a little while.

Beatrice Cook's husband, Everett, didn't like the way his kitchen had been taken over. Beatrice had welcomed her stupid multicultural club students to their house and hadn't even told him they were coming over. She'd probably known that if she'd asked, he would have said no, would have suggested they cook in the school cafeteria instead. But here they were, and Beatrice had even gone out and bought cupcakes and bottles of Coke and Sprite for the kids, and it looked like they were having a party in his kitchen.

Beatrice's students were making a mess. They had flour on their hands and were touching the counter and cabinets and faucet and leaving crusty fingerprints all over. There were eight or nine kids and they were all sorts of colors and looked like misfits. Nerds and geeks. Not the type of kids he would have been friends with in high school.

He looked at his wife mixing up a bowl of dough, thought about how they only had a few weeks before their baby would be born, and wondered what he'd do if his kid turned out to be a loser. He couldn't have a loser for a kid, especially if the kid was a boy. But Beatrice, well, she didn't care. She said she'd love the kid no matter what, whether it was a loser or a retard or liked math.

Everett said, "Excuse me," and pushed past a chubby boy he'd heard Beatrice call Rigoberto. Rigoberto was giving a lecture on something called empanadas, and Beatrice seemed to actually be interested in what he was saying. Everett just wanted a goddamned beer from his own refrigerator, and he had to pass through this gauntlet of kids to get one.

"Sparrow, would you get the oregano out of the cabinet on the left?" Beatrice said.

Sparrow? Who named their kid Sparrow? A tall, thin, brown-skinned boy wearing a Green Day T-shirt moved toward the cabinet. Everett took a bottle of Budweiser out of the refrigerator. Beatrice shook her head. She mouthed, *No beer in front of the students.* Everett pretended he didn't understand what she said and opened the beer and tossed the cap on the counter. He stood in Sparrow's way as he returned with the oregano.

"You ever been to one of their concerts?" he said, pointing at Sparrow's shirt.

The boy shook his head.

"No?" said Everett. "You're missing out. I saw them at Lollapalooza."

The boy blinked a few times, then tried to get around him.

"Hello?" said Everett, waving a hand in front of the boy's face. "Do you speak English?"

"Everett, please," said Beatrice. "We're trying to work here. Could you maybe go somewhere else?"

"Fine," Everett said. "I was just thirsty." He'd only taken one sip of his beer, but he returned to the refrigerator and took out two more bottles. He made sure the three bottles clinked loudly in his hands as he walked out of the kitchen. In the TV room down the hall, he picked up the remote and set the beers down. There was nothing interesting on TV, so he pressed Play on the VCR to see what Beatrice had recorded. It was that stupid show, *Friends*, that she loved. Everett watched and felt jealous of the lives the characters led. It was all made up, he knew that, but there were these people on it who weren't much older than he was. They lived in New York City and everything was fun for them. They didn't have unwanted babies on the way. They didn't have real responsibilities. The characters' lives were so different from his. Even though he never really got any roles, Joey was an actor; he didn't have a dull job like Everett's. Everett was an equipment operator trainee for the Kansas Department of Transportation. He thought he'd rather go to auditions than maintain the highways, paint lines on the roads, work the motor graders and compactors. He'd never acted in his life, but acting sounded far easier than his job. On *Friends*, Monica was a chef and that nerd Ross was a paleontologist. What would it be like to be a chef? A paleontologist? Everett had loved playing with his plastic dinosaurs when he was a little boy. Maybe he would have liked being a paleontologist. If he were a paleontologist, maybe he could go far away, go dig and dig, let dirt build up under his fingernails, allow holes to wear through the knees of his pants. He could forget all about assembling a crib and mowing the lawn and taking his boots off at the entranceway to his house so he didn't stain the cream-colored carpet.

If you lived in New York City and could hang out with your friends for hours each day in a coffee shop, the last thing that would cross your mind was babies. Ross had a kid on *Friends*, but it lived with his ex-wife, so he didn't really have to think about it. Soon Everett would have to think about a baby all the time; he'd have to worry about money and make sure the baby had what it needed. He was twenty-four years old. He wasn't ready to be a father. He wasn't even sure he wanted to be married anymore. He was tired of Beatrice and her bossiness, her perfectionism. This life was too much for him, too much too soon. He wanted to get into one of the big paving trucks from work, the compactor with the enormous wheel, roll over everything about his life, start fresh and smooth.

"Where were you and Wendell last night?" Lily demanded. "We worked so hard at Mrs. Cook's."

Priti hated Lily. Just because they'd once been friends, it didn't mean that Priti owed her any explanations. Lily stood with her arms crossed next to a fake ficus tree with dust on its leaves in the lobby of the nursing home. Priti didn't want to be here, but she felt guilty about missing the cooking the night before.

"Now you're going to get credit for the food, and you had nothing to do with making it," Lily said.

"Do you want me to leave?" Priti said.

"No," Priya said. "Stay. You're here already. And besides, we don't have a car here."

Priti glared at her sister. She didn't need Priya trying to stick up for her.

"You could just leave with Wendell," Lily said. "I hope you guys had fun last night."

"Totally," Priti said. "I can't wait for you to meet Wendell Junior in nine months. Will you be the godmother?"

Lily took a step back, scandalized. "Can you believe her?" she said, turning to Priya.

"Shhh," Priya said. "Mrs. Cook's talking." Mrs. Cook was at the front of the dining room explaining to the small group of senior citizens who'd gathered about Things Inside of Other Things. She told them she hoped this would be a wonderful way for the Half and Half Club to share their heritages. An old man with enormous glasses and a puff of white hair stood up while Mrs. Cook was still talking and shuffled to the table in the corner that was covered in plates of the food they'd prepared. He picked up a dumpling with his fingers and ate it in one bite. The rest of the old people in the room flocked to the table and began to scavenge.

"Oh, these are too spicy!" said a woman in a pink sweatshirt adorned with an image of kittens piled in a wicker basket. She put down a samosa that Priti was sure Priya had made the night before. The samosa sat on the edge of the table with a bite taken out of it. Priti could see the turmeric-stained potatoes inside and fought an urge to march up to the woman and tell her to finish the samosa her sister had made. She looked at Priya, who had a tight, fake smile on her face, and Priti could tell Priya was trying to act like she didn't care what the woman had said. Priti knew how much pride Priya took in every damn thing she did, how she wanted everything to be perfect, and she knew Priya would take the woman's comment far too seriously. She'd be upset with herself for several days for using too many chilies.

"She's probably just not used to eating anything with flavor," Priti whispered to Priya. Priya didn't respond.

"These old white people are beasts," said Rigoberto. "Look at them eat!"

"I was hoping that each member of the Half and Half Club could come up and explain the cultural significance of their food item," said Mrs. Cook, but none of the old people were listening to her. "I've got plastic forks," she said quietly. "At least you might want to use a fork."

"I brought chopsticks," Lily said, marching to the front of the room. "I don't suppose anyone wants to learn to use them?"

Priti looked at Wendell, who'd moved near the door and stood by the idiot football coach, Mr. Cooper. Why in the world was Mr. Cooper even here? He'd hardly said anything all day, and as far as Priti could figure, he'd just been asked to come so he could unload the food from Mrs. Cook's car. He'd sulked, and it was obvious that he hadn't wanted to be at the nursing home. Maybe he was grossed out by old people. Priti tried to smile at Wendell, but he wouldn't make eye contact. She saw Mr. Cooper put his arm around Wendell, saw him pat his back and then his side. It was the sort of thing coaches did, a way to get their players moving. But Wendell didn't move; he just slumped against the wall.

Last night hadn't gone the way Priti had expected. They'd gotten into Wendell's car and Priti asked Wendell whether he wanted to go for a ride before going to Mrs. Cook's house. He'd agreed, and she'd directed him to a wide, flat field where they could park and no one would bother them. She'd been there with boys before. Priti had moved closer to Wendell in the front seat, but he'd put up a hand, then he'd begun to cry. "Are you hurt or something?" she said.

Wendell shook his head. "No. Well, yes. I mean, I'm not in pain now, but I'm hurt."

She didn't know what he meant, but she nodded.

"Look," he said. He unbuttoned his shirt, took his right arm out of its sleeve, and turned his back to her. Pink, raised scars ran across his shoulder and upper back. It looked like he'd had surgery. He pulled his arm back into the sleeve and buttoned the shirt back up. "Me and Sparrow, we were skateboarding this summer. Up at the reservoir when there was the drought. It was so dry that we could skate right into it. We were going crazy trying all these tricks, and I was doing this coffin trick where you go from standing on your skateboard to lying down on it while the skateboard is still moving, like you're a dead guy in a coffin. I fell and tore my labrum. It basically means I ripped the cartilage in my shoulder socket to shreds, totally tore it off the bone."

"But you can still use your arm, right?" Once she said it, she realized what the problem was. If Wendell was a normal person, he'd be fine. But he was a baseball star, the best player on the team. He was a senior, and recruiters had been watching him pitch for the past few years. Everyone assumed he'd get a baseball scholarship. Priti knew his family didn't have much money; the scholarship might be the only way he could go to college.

"I'm no good anymore," he said. "I can't pitch."

"But you'll recover, right?"

"The doctor says it won't ever be like it was before. And even if I feel like I can pitch, there's a high risk of tearing it again."

He wept then, and Priti moved closer. She wrapped her arms around him, let him cry on her shoulder until she could feel her shirt getting wet. She patted his back, running her hand up and down his

spine, the way she did the one time she babysat her little cousin Ra-
jiv and he wouldn't stop sobbing. She held Wendell until he sat up
straight and wiped his eyes with his palms. "I went to the doctor this
afternoon," he said. "He told me I shouldn't play baseball again." He
seemed embarrassed, turned his head and sniffled as he looked out
the window. The window fogged from his breath.

"I have an idea," Priti said. "Where are the potatoes?"

"They're raw," said Wendell. "You want a raw potato?"

Priti nodded, and they got out of the car. Wendell opened the
trunk. A large brown bag of russet potatoes rested in the trunk. "My
mom brought these home from work for the pierogies," Wendell said.

Wendell's mother worked at the Burger Shack on Carpenter Street.
She'd worked there for as long as Priti could remember. She wondered if Wendell's mother had been allowed to take the potatoes or
whether she'd dragged the bag out the door without permission. Priti
ripped open the top of the bag. She took out two potatoes and handed
one to Wendell. "Throw it," she said.

"Throw it where?"

"Anywhere," Priti said, her hand sweeping across the field.

"I can't throw with my right arm anymore," Wendell said, turning
the potato around and around in his hands.

"So throw with your left."

Wendell tossed the potato hard, and it landed out of sight. Even
with his left arm, Wendell was powerful. Priti wondered how good he
could have become if he hadn't gotten hurt. She handed him another
potato, and he threw again, and this potato disappeared too. She threw
one, but it only went a few feet and thunked into the tall grass. They
hauled the bag out of the trunk and brought it to the middle of the
field. Then they threw until there were no more potatoes left to throw.

"We have a problem," said Dr. Hargrave. They'd all been summoned
to his office. Danny and Beatrice stood while Sparrow, Wendell, and
Rigoberto sat in chairs in front of Dr. Hargrave's desk. Danny looked

down at the tops of the three boys' heads. They all had so much hair. It wasn't fair. But maybe they, too, would begin to bald by nineteen, be nearly bald by twenty-five. Life worked in mysterious ways.

It was Monday morning, the day after the visit to Sun Meadow Senior Home. As they had been packing up to leave the nursing home the night before, an old woman with a voice like a whirring drill shouted out that her engagement ring from 1934 was missing from the nightstand by her bed. The Half and Half Club was asked to wait while the premises were searched. Another woman discovered her pearl necklace was missing, and another was missing a locket. A man said his pocket watch had disappeared and declared that it had been bequeathed to him by his best friend who'd been a train conductor.

"It just can't be possible that my students had anything to do with this," said Beatrice. "They're good kids."

The director of the nursing home sent the residents back to their rooms, asked them to search carefully. The nurses joined the search. The missing items did not turn up.

"We should search the kids," Danny said. "If we refuse, they might call the police."

And so they'd searched, Beatrice checking the girls' pockets and handbags, Danny patting down the boys as if he were a cop. He pulled the engagement ring out of Sparrow's pocket, the pearls out of Wendell's windbreaker, and the locket out of the back pocket of Rigoberto's baggy cargo pants. Beatrice had begged for leniency. She asked the nursing home director not to call the police. She said she'd tell the school's principal and he'd discipline them.

"At the least they owe the people they stole from apologies," said the director of the nursing home.

"I didn't take that necklace," said Rigoberto. "I've never even seen it before!"

"You have to apologize," Beatrice said.

And so they did, Rigoberto and Wendell each choking out an apology to the owners of the jewelry that had been found in their pockets.

Sparrow didn't say anything, and tears filled his eyes, and for a moment Danny felt a fizzle of guilt in his belly.

"Could Sparrow write you a letter?" Beatrice asked the owner of the engagement ring. "He's a lovely writer."

"I don't want anything from him," the woman with the drill voice said. "Just go away."

"My pocket watch," said the man. "You didn't find my pocket watch."

Danny reached into the pocket of his blazer and curled his fingers around the pocket watch that rested heavily there. He hoped it hadn't been wound but thought he maybe heard ticking. "I'm sorry," said Danny. "I really am. None of these boys have it."

When Beatrice and the students had been setting up, heating the food in the kitchen, opening packages of napkins and plastic utensils and paper plates, Danny had roamed the halls unseen. People were around, but no one noticed him. That's how it was now. He was inoffensive looking, pale and bland, and he knew his bald head and round face made him look innocent, like someone people should feel a little sorry for. Women no longer looked at him the way they used to. He slipped into room after room in the nursing home. They were all empty. Oldies music seeped from the recreation room down the hall, and he heard an instructor shouting out exercise directions, asking the seniors to step to the left, raise their arms, step to the right. He'd entered seven rooms and had taken an object from each room. He'd dropped the items into his blazer's pockets. Then he'd patted each boy on the back, a gesture he'd developed in his time coaching. It could be a sympathetic pat, an encouraging pat, even an angry pat. It had been so easy to pat the boys and distract them so he could slip the jewelry into their pockets.

He'd wanted to cause trouble. He was angry with Beatrice and wanted to ruin her little community service trip. He'd called her house in the morning, and her husband had picked up and said Beatrice was in the shower. Danny lied to Everett and said his car had broken down. Could Beatrice maybe give him a ride to the nursing home? He'd given Everett directions to his house—even though he knew Beatrice would not need them—and told him he'd wait outside at 11 a.m.

"So you got dragged into this dumbass field trip, too?" Everett had said.

"Yeah, the principal said I had to go," said Danny. He thought of all the things Beatrice had told him about Everett, about his temper, his impatience.

"Glad I get to stay home and watch football," Everett said. Something that sounded like a snort came through the line.

"Lucky man," Danny said. "You're a lucky man."

When Beatrice had pulled up outside his house, she'd been furious. "I can't believe you called my house and talked to my husband. It's not appropriate, Danny."

"I thought fate may have pushed us back together."

"Dr. Hargrave pushed us together. That's all."

"But the baby—"

"We're not having this discussion. Not again," she said, and clamped her lips shut.

It had started about a year ago, both of them lingering when everyone else had left after faculty happy hour at the Thirsty Guernsey Pub. They'd both had too much to drink already, and Danny ordered another pitcher of beer, which they drained over the next hour. Danny told her how hard it was to be back in Sun Meadow, how tortured he felt as a coach. He looked at the boys, so young and powerful and full of potential, and felt pulsating jealousy. He revealed that numbers confused him now, and he didn't know how he'd get through teaching his classes; he'd once been good at math, but now equations and formulas and proofs made a nonsensical whirl in his brain. Beatrice told Danny about her husband, Everett, whom she regretted marrying when she was so young. She'd married him because that's what everyone did in Sun Meadow; they got married young, had families, and stayed in Sun Meadow forever. Everett wasn't terrible to her, but he often acted bored or angry when they were together, said he wished he could have more fun, spend more time with his friends. She said she thought there was more out in the world for her. She wanted to travel or maybe go back to school to study music. After they'd finished the beer and drunkenly confessed so much to each other, they'd walked the mile to Danny's house and Beatrice had paused for a minute before entering the threshold. But then she'd let Danny lead her to his bedroom and then Danny knew there was no turning back.

Danny had fallen in love with her. He'd known it was stupid to fall for a married woman, but he couldn't stop his heart from feeling what it felt. He'd only experienced love once before, and that had been Nicole in college, who'd broken his heart for the first time. They'd met during freshman orientation; she lived one floor above him in his dorm. He'd fallen for her immediately because she was so different from any girl he'd known in Sun Meadow. He gave her the full Danny Cooper charisma treatment: he wrote her hastily dashed-off poems that he knew were terrible but hoped were charming in their terribleness, bought her small trinkets from the campus bookstore and left them outside her dorm room door, showed up outside her classrooms as each class ended and walked with her across campus, and always flashed her his wide smile that no girls in Sun Meadow had ever been able to resist. Nicole was from Kansas City and had spent her junior year of high school in Paris and was fluent in French. She had a small diamond stud in her nose and a pile of French movies on VHS tapes in her dorm room and had even brought her own VCR to school. She was the most sophisticated person Danny had ever met, and for her, he would even sit through those boring subtitled movies and then try to talk to her about them afterwards. He'd brought her home for Thanksgiving, and his mother had been smitten by her beauty and good manners and had whispered to Danny, "Even though she has a nose ring, I like her the best of all of the girls." His father had brought Nicole to the den and showed her a wall lined with photos of Danny in football uniforms throughout the years above dozens of football trophies crowded on top of a bookshelf. She'd run her fingers over the trophies, leaned in close to examine each photo.

Once they returned to campus, Nicole acted strange toward him, distant. When he'd pressed her about what was wrong, she said, "Everything is football with you. Going to your house made me realize that. And—" She stopped.

"What?" Danny said. "What's wrong?"

"Well, it's not like you've gotten to play here. Who are you without football? What if football doesn't work out for you? What then?" She'd come to the games throughout the fall, and during each game he'd sat on the bench the entire time. Sometimes he'd look back and search the stands, and when he found Nicole, she'd have a Styrofoam cup of hot chocolate in one hand and a paperback in the other, and he realized now that she'd only come to the games out of some sense of duty.

"I don't know who I am," Danny said. He wished he had a better answer. He wished he could say that he would direct movies or be an architect or a dolphin trainer if football didn't work out. But football was all he knew, and before he'd had the chance to figure it out, Nicole had figured out that without football he was no one, nobody.

They'd gone their separate ways for winter break, and when they returned to campus for the spring semester, Nicole told him that she'd met someone, Alejandro, an exchange student from Spain. She said that Alejandro was worldly, knew about wine and art and music and film. Danny wanted to cry when she said the word "film." No one said "film" in Sun Meadow; everyone said "movies." And maybe Nicole was right; maybe all Danny had ever known of the world was cleats and shoulder pads and goalposts and playbooks.

At spring practice a few weeks later, he couldn't keep up with the other players—falling behind even the three-hundred-pound offensive linemen—while running wind sprints, and when his coach asked what was wrong, he said he was heartbroken.

"You been diagnosed with a heart murmur?" the coach asked. "Heart disease run in your family?"

"No, Coach, I mean, my heart's broken. Nicole broke up with me."

Coach looked at him and shook his head. "We're not talking a physical ailment here?" he said.

"No," said Danny. "But I just can't run or pass or keep the plays straight in my head because of my heart."

"I don't want to hear excuses," Coach said. "You haven't proved yourself all year. Don't give me that Nicole bullshit."

By his sophomore year he'd quit football altogether, and he spent the next three years thinking alternately of football and of Nicole and what could have been. He felt like a failure, and the only solace he could find was in his math classes, where he could escape into complex equations and forget about the people that surrounded him.

He thought Beatrice would be the woman to heal him, but Beatrice had called things off when she learned she was pregnant. "It's mine, isn't it?" Danny had said, and Beatrice had conceded that it was possible. "We'll run away together," he told her, and she shook her head. "It doesn't matter if it's mine or not. I'll love it either way," he said, although he felt sure that it was his and that it was a boy and that he would teach the boy to play football and grow up strong and noble.

But she said no, said that this was a sign from God that she had to return to Everett, that she had to be faithful. She said Danny was not to ever talk to her outside of a professional capacity ever again.

"It's over all of a sudden? Just like that?" he'd said.

"Just like that," she'd said.

In the car on the way to the nursing home, he hoped she'd remember their spark, but she just stared forward, turned up the radio, and acted as if there was no one in the passenger seat. "Mr. Jones" by Counting Crows came on the radio, and Beatrice sang along.

"This is our chance," Danny said. "Keep driving. Let's go away and never come back." He'd withdrawn almost all the money from his savings account in hundred-dollar bills and had stuffed as many as he could into his wallet. He'd wanted to be prepared if she said yes. Now, sitting in the car, he could feel the too-thick wallet pressing into his right butt cheek.

"Don't be stupid," Beatrice said.

Danny wanted to scream, to pull the steering wheel so they'd roll off the road into a ravine. But he did nothing. In the car, he'd decided it was his fate to suffer a quiet, loveless life; maybe he was being punished for his fickleness with girls in high school. But a few hours later in the nursing home, he'd seen the jewelry in the seniors' rooms and wanted so badly to ruin the day, to do something horrible. He was tired of suffering silently.

"Community service," said Dr. Hargrave, pointing at each of the boys. "For all of you. For the rest of the school year, you'll each spend ten hours a week volunteering at the nursing home. You'll do anything they want. Mop the floors, take out the trash, play board games with the residents."

"They hate us there," said Wendell. "They think we're thieves."

"You *are* thieves," said Dr. Hargrave. "How else do you explain what was in your pockets?"

"Maybe one of the residents put the jewelry in their pockets," Danny said. "It's possible. They're good boys. I've had them all in class and have never had a disciplinary problem with any of them."

Dr. Hargrave glared at him. Danny tried to match his glare. He wanted to save these boys, to admit what he'd done, but he couldn't lose his job. It was all he had now.

"O-o-once I stole," said Sparrow. "I was th-th-three. A visitor to our tribe left a s-s-skiff by the bank of the river, and I got in it because the skiff was green and shiny and I thought it was beautiful. I laid down in it and floated for half a day. I had no oars and just drifted, looking at the shapes of the clouds. Another tribe saw me and pulled the boat to shore and said I couldn't go home because I was a thief for stealing the boat. They chopped up the boat for firewood. I was there for a week and they didn't feed me. I ate ants, which I remember tasted like lemons. One night I stole another skiff from that tribe and the currents were moving in the right direction and I floated back home. But at home I was called a thief too, for stealing from the other tribe, and none of the other children were allowed to play with me. All I'd wanted was to take a boat ride. I stole two skiffs when I was three, but I didn't steal the ring. The ring wasn't something that was beautiful to me or something I needed."

Danny had never heard Sparrow say so much. "Is that why you were put up for adoption? Because they thought you were a thief?" Now both Dr. Hargrave and Beatrice glared at him, but he didn't care. He wanted to know.

"Th-th-that's a different story," said Sparrow.

"What if instead of working at the nursing home, the guys help out with the football team, with equipment and stuff?" Danny said. He'd lost his mind at the nursing home and had done something cruel and unnecessary. The boys were innocent. It had been Beatrice all along that he'd wanted to destroy. He'd made a terrible mistake. And worst of all, the last thing that needed to happen in Sun Meadow, which could be a kind of closed-minded place, was for people to think these kids—these half-and-half kids—were criminals.

"The punishment should match the crime. I'd hardly say being a football booster is a punishment," said Dr. Hargrave. He fixed his stare on the boys, and Danny was impressed that he seemed able to glare at all three of them simultaneously. "You should be happy about community service. You're lucky no one pressed charges. With something like this on your records, it would be difficult to get into college."

"I'm not going to college," spat Wendell. "So whatever."

"That's a poor attitude, young man," said Dr. Hargrave.

"I hope you boys have learned a lesson," said Beatrice. She sounded so awful, so bossy and pretentious saying it, as if she was sure the boys were thieves. But then, she was always sure she was right. Always.

Danny's hand curled around the pocket watch in his blazer pocket. If his life had to be miserable, hers should be too. He wondered when Beatrice would empty the light blue purse she'd brought to the nursing home and left leaning against a wall in the dining room all afternoon. When she did, she'd find other things that had been pilfered from the residents' rooms. These were not objects the residents had noticed missing right away, these were not precious things. When she looked in the bag, she'd find a set of false teeth, a dirty sock, and a bright green false eye.

It was a message from God, loud and clear. God had sent Danny Cooper to test Mrs. Cook, and she had failed, had committed sins of the flesh. She'd been tempted to run away with him when he'd suggested it in the car. They could go far from Sun Meadow, escape to somewhere foggy and gray, mountainous, somewhere totally different. They could start a new life with the baby. But she had stayed strong, had said no. Then in Dr. Hargrave's office her heart had swelled when Danny offered to let the boys help out with the football team. What charity and grace, she'd thought. He would reform the boys, teach them to be decent again. She thought then of how he would be a good father.

But then she'd reached into her purse on her drive home from school, feeling for her Chapstick, and had found instead a round, hard object. A glass eye. The eye was green, the same color as her eyes. Danny had always complimented her eyes, said they were the color of the clover in the field where, when he had barely learned to walk, his father had taught him to play football. She pulled her car over and rifled through her purse. She found a dirty sock and a pair of dentures stuffed under her tissues and hair scrunchies and makeup. She suddenly understood it all: Danny had committed the sin, Danny had stolen, Danny had left the eye as a nasty, mean message. The boys, her boys—Sparrow and Wendell and Rigoberto—were good, honest kids, and now everyone thought of them as thieves. Danny had slipped those things into their pockets, just as he had slipped those awful objects into her purse. She was sure of this in a way that she hadn't been sure of anything in months. She filled with rage, and her hands shook on the steering wheel. She forced herself to breathe slowly and steadily, to calm herself; she knew anger was not good for the baby.

As soon as she stepped inside her house, Mrs. Cook decided she would disappoint God no longer. The glass eye was precisely the sign she needed. It reminded her that God saw everything, knew about all the ways in which she'd sinned. She put the eye and the dentures and the sock in a plastic grocery bag, tied a tight knot on top, and brought the bag out to the trash can in the garage. She slammed the door when she returned inside, and sat at the kitchen table clutching her head in her hands. She was finished with Danny, and she wouldn't even allow herself to think about him, to wonder what life might be like with him instead of Everett. She'd spent far too much time contemplating such things in the months since she'd learned she was pregnant.

She vowed she would change. She would start going to church again. For so many years she'd been faithful, had lived true to the word of the Bible, but in the last few years she and Everett had stopped going to church. Instead, Everett watched sports all day on Sunday. It didn't matter what sport was on, he just collapsed on the couch, eyes glued to the screen, eating an entire pizza over the course of the afternoon. She spent Sundays grading papers and feeling resentful toward Everett. But all this would change. She would force Everett to go to church again. They'd eat dinner together every night at the kitchen table with the TV turned off. They'd tell each other about their days. She'd try to remember what it was she'd liked about him when they'd married when they were both nineteen. She'd force him to be a good father. She'd be a good mother and, more important, a good wife.

When Everett returned from work that afternoon, he was grumpy and didn't want to talk to her. He turned on the TV, stared at it, and ate an entire box of granola bars for dinner. By eleven, Everett was in bed fast asleep. Mrs. Cook walked into the kitchen. She opened the refrigerator and took out bologna, American cheese, mayonnaise. She assembled a sandwich, wrapped it in aluminum foil, and put it into a plastic shopping bag from Walmart. Didn't Everett have some sort of lunchbox, something metal and sturdy? She hadn't seen it in years. She hadn't thought in a long time about what he ate for lunch. Mrs. Cook added an apple to the bag, then poured some cheese crackers into a Ziploc bag and added that too. She put in a can of Coke and then another; surely Everett got thirsty with all the hard labor he did. She placed a napkin on top of it all and put the Walmart bag in the refrigerator. In the morning, she'd tell Everett that she made him lunch, and maybe he'd smile, maybe he'd be grateful. And then the next day she'd make him lunch again and she'd do the same the day after that. And they would go on this way, and God would smile down upon them and bless them with a beautiful, loving child, a child who looked just like Everett, a child who was, without a doubt, Everett's. *We will be OK, we will be OK, we will be OK*, Mrs. Cook thought. She tried to convince herself that this was true, and headed upstairs to bed.

"Get up," Priti said.

Priya opened her eyes. It was 1 a.m. Her sister had snuck into her room and was wearing all black again: black boots, black jeans, black sweatshirt, and black eyeliner. Priya wondered whether Priti was about to head out to some secret late-night party. Maybe Priti would ask Priya to cover for her, to make up a complicated lie if their parents woke up and found her missing. "What do you want?" Priya said.

"Wendell said he didn't steal the pearls."

"Why are you telling me this now? Is Wendell your boyfriend?"

"No," Priti said, shaking her head. "But he's my friend."

"I didn't think you were capable of being friends with boys."

"First time for everything."

Priya stared up at the ceiling. "Couldn't you have told me this tomorrow?"

"I think Mr. Cooper stole the jewelry."

"Mr. Cooper's a teacher."

"Oh, and teachers never do anything wrong? Teachers are angels?"

"Why would he do that? It doesn't make sense," Priya said. "Why would he steal it then put it in other people's pockets?"

"You think Sparrow would steal?"

"No," Priti said. "I know he wouldn't. He's good."

"I saw Mr. Cooper patting Wendell at the nursing home, kind of slipping his hand in his pocket."

"That's crazy."

Priti nodded. "He's crazy. I think this is what happens when high school is the best part of your life."

"Isn't high school the best part of your life?"

"God, I hope not," Priti said. "That would suck."

Priya was surprised to hear this. She'd thought Priti loved her life, loved being the wild and free and popular one. It had never occurred to her that Priti hoped for more than what she had right now. "So what do you want to do? Are you going to egg Mr. Cooper's house or something? Slash his tires?"

Priti shook her head. "Let's bury the rabbits. I took two shovels out of the garage before dinner. They're leaning against the big tree outside."

"Really?" said Priya. Why would her sister want to do this? She knew Priti thought the rabbits were disgusting. Was this—in some strange way—an apology?

"Yeah," said Priti. "And we'll find the Sandersons' dog and lock him back in their yard. I feel bad for Sparrow. I know he didn't steal. And I know he loves that dog." She held out a fist to Priya then unfurled her fingers. A silver object was dimly illuminated by the streetlight outside. "It's a dog whistle. He'll come running."

"But then he'll howl again and you won't be able to sleep."

"Maybe he won't howl. Maybe he got out his wildness and now he'll be OK."

"Can that happen?" said Priya.

"I think so," Priti said. Then she flexed her arms as if she were a cartoon superhero and said in a mock serious voice, "We'll restore peace to the neighborhood." She slid the whistle into the pocket of her jeans and looked down at Priya, who still lay in bed.

Priya was reminded of when they were very little, when Priti woke her up in the middle of the night when no one else was awake and the house was dark. Although they'd shared a room then, they'd each had their own small bed. When they were young, Priti had nightmares. In the middle of the night, almost every night, Priti would shake Priya's shoulder, stand by the side of her bed breathing steadily in the quiet stillness of the darkened room, and once Priya said, "OK," Priti would crawl into Priya's bed, push her warm body next to Priya's. Priya would move her pillow so they could share it, each taking half, their heads so close their ears touched. It was only after Priti was tucked into Priya's bed that she could sleep through the night; only then would the night-mares fade away.

Priya got out of bed. She put on black jeans and a hooded black sweatshirt, an outfit that was almost identical to her sister's. She pulled on dark socks and laced her black boots. "OK," she said. Priti slid open the window, and they slipped into the darkness.

THE FLANNERY O'CONNOR AWARD FOR SHORT FICTION

David Walton, *Evening Out*

Leigh Allison Wilson, *From the Bottom Up*

Sandra Thompson, *Close-Ups*

Susan Neville, *The Invention of Flight*

Mary Hood, *How Far She Went*

François Camoin, *Why Men Are Afraid of Women*

Molly Giles, *Rough Translations*

Daniel Curley, *Living with Snakes*

Peter Meinke, *The Piano Tuner*

Tony Ardizzone, *The Evening News*

Salvatore La Puma, *The Boys of Bensonhurst*

Melissa Pritchard, *Spirit Seizures*

Philip F. Deaver, *Silent Retreats*

Gail Galloway Adams, *The Purchase of Order*

Carole L. Glickfeld, *Useful Gifts*

Antonya Nelson, *The Expendables*

Nancy Zafris, *The People I Know*

Debra Monroe, *The Source of Trouble*

Robert H. Abel, *Ghost Traps*

T. M. McNally, *Low Flying Aircraft*

Alfred DePew, *The Melancholy of Departure*

Dennis Hathaway, *The Consequences of Desire*

Rita Ciresi, *Mother Rocket*

Dianne Nelson, *A Brief History of Male Nudes in America*

Christopher McIlroy, *All My Relations*

Alyce Miller, *The Nature of Longing*

Carol Lee Lorenzo, *Nervous Dancer*

C. M. Mayo, *Sky over El Nido*